A W

You are cordi...   ...e

Heiress Ivy Je...   —
Manhattan's l...
at New York's *ultimate* wedding venue: Parker &
Parker.

With their guest list a Who's Who of the city's
A-listers, Ivy and Sebastian want a wedding to
remember! So they need the best in the business
to help plan their perfect day... Cue Alexandra
Harris, Hailey Thomas and Autumn Jones! The
wedding planner, florist and maid of honor may be
there to make Ivy and Sebastian's day magical...
but what if their love lives receive a sprinkle of
Christmas magic, too?

Discover Alexandra and Drew's story in

The Wedding Planner's Christmas Wish
by Cara Colter

Available now!

And look out for the next two books in the trilogy

Hailey and Giovanni's story by Ellie Darkins
and
Autumn and Jack's story by Susan Meier

Coming soon!

Dear Reader,

Like so many of you, I have been traveling a hard road. On a personal level, my family has been hit over and over again with tragedy. Two terrible and separate accidents in a very short span of time left us all reeling. There has been a heartbreaking diagnosis. The loyal dog who had lain at my feet, snoring softly through the creation of over thirty books, crossed over to the other side.

Add to this a troubled and strange world, where the rules change daily. Sometimes, it feels as if we may never know normal again.

I do not feel as if I am getting through any of this with courage, or grace. But I am getting through it. What has helped me the most? The story. Always it is the story. I am so profoundly grateful to the authors who continue to weave their magic and invite me to escape into the marvelous worlds of their creation.

As I write, this is my intention: let these words bring a glimmer of hope.

I am deeply grateful to you, the reader, for allowing me the great privilege of serving you with my words, with the story.

Always,

Cara

The Wedding Planner's Christmas Wish

Cara Colter

HARLEQUIN

Romance

Special thanks and acknowledgment are given to
Cara Colter for her contribution to the
Wedding in New York miniseries.

Recycling programs
for this product may
not exist in your area.

ISBN-13: 978-1-335-40683-5

The Wedding Planner's Christmas Wish

For questions and comments about the quality of this book,
please contact us at CustomerService@Harlequin.com.

Harlequin Enterprises ULC
22 Adelaide St. West, 40th Floor
Toronto, Ontario M5H 4E3, Canada
www.Harlequin.com

Printed in U.S.A.

Cara Colter shares her home in beautiful British Columbia, Canada, with her husband of more than thirty years, an ancient, crabby cat, and several horses. She has three grown children, and two grandsons.

To Tessa Avon

With deepest gratitude for the hope you have
brought to so many hearts.

Praise for
Cara Colter

"Ms. Colter's writing style is one you will want
to continue to read. Her descriptions place you
there.... This story does have a[n] HEA but leaves
you wanting more."

—*Harlequin Junkie* on *His Convenient Royal Bride*

CHAPTER ONE

ALEXANDRA HARRIS HAD an excellent imagination, so if there was one thing she loved—but rarely got to experience—it was when things were actually *better* than she imagined them.

Parker and Parker was just that: better than she'd imagined.

Located at the edge of New York City's Central Park, the soaring Renaissance-style facade of the building made it look like a gorgeous mansion, almost but not quite castle-like.

"Just like a fairy tale," she whispered, not unaware of a feeling of homecoming. Fairy tales, professionally if not personally, were, after all, Alexandra's specialty. There was a reason she and her company, Ever After, were currently New York's most in-demand wedding planners.

She passed through a black wrought-iron gate that was bordered on both sides by a high, well-manicured hedge that was, this first day of October, just beginning to take on the bold colors of autumn. But as glorious as those colors were,

Alexandra imagined how it all would look in two and a half months, when the hedge would be leafless but ten times as magical, decorated and lit with a million tiny white lights, not just for Christmas, but for the wedding of the century.

Two and a half months might seem like a long time to most people, but Alexandra was aware how fast that final lead-up time to the wedding would go.

Ivy Jenkins, heiress to the billion-dollar business Jenkins Inc., and Sebastian Davis, CEO of New York's most exciting tech start-up, were tying the knot.

And they'd asked her, Alexandra Harris, to be the wedding planner for their unforgettable Christmas-themed wedding.

Christmas, she told herself, something she was also good at professionally, if not personally. That unshakable feeling of dread...

She ordered herself, firmly, to stop it. She had a wedding that would take one hundred percent of her focus, thank goodness.

Because it had to be perfect. Having the rich and famous fight to hire you came with pressures. These people, with their wealth and influence, could make you with a word. And just as easily break you.

A career always hung on that impossible pursuit of absolute perfection. Alexandra was aware she was always one disaster—or even one tiny bridal disappointment—away from being ruined.

And so in her quest to constantly up her game—and particularly for this wedding—Alexandra had set her sights on Parker and Parker. She'd known instantly it was the only venue that would do. She'd been stunned when Gabe Evans, the head of events for the gorgeous old Jacobean-style castle, built in 1831, had told her they didn't take weddings.

How could they not take weddings when it was so perfect? Parker and Parker was made for weddings!

But no, he'd insisted that the venue in general—and the owner of the venue in particular, Drew Parker—preferred conferences and events and had made them their specialty.

Conferences? Congregations of boring pediatricians or neuroscientists or whatever other professional group could afford the steep fees? Events? Like stuffy charity balls and mind-numbing auctions for good causes? All right, at least events might be noble. But still, they had nothing on the pure charm of a blissful wedding day!

Alexandra hadn't achieved her success as a dream weaver and fairy-tale provider by taking no for an answer.

Despite time pressures—she had to nail down the venue—she'd kept at Gabe until he'd been persuaded. Now, standing here on the grounds, she knew her persistence had been well worth it. Nothing could be more perfect than this! In an hour or so, Ivy and Sebastian were going to get here and see it for the first time, the extraordinary place that would provide that essential backdrop to build the rest of their day—and the beginning of their life together—around.

Today, she'd meet Gabe in person for the first time, which was a relief. She had the check for the deposit in her purse. Gabe had confirmed for December 14, and the days leading up to it, of course, and they had long since completed the contract using an online signing service.

Even so, Alexandra had experienced a strange sense of him ducking actually meeting her. She wasn't sure why he made her a bit uneasy. On the phone, and in emails and texts, he always seemed gracious and even enthusiastic about the wedding.

And yet, sometimes, he seemed distracted when they spoke. Scheduled emails arrived late. Phone calls were forgotten. Somehow, her dealings with Gabe had an odd feeling of subterfuge. There were even times when she spoke to him that it actually felt as if he was whispering.

But here, on the grounds, with the check in her purse, she dismissed her anxieties. They were as normal for her as they were for the bride—maybe even more so. It was Alexandra's job to worry about everything that could go wrong and fix it before it even surfaced as a problem.

But, finally, she was here, and finally, it felt real. She couldn't wait to explore the property with Gabe, inspect the facilities and kitchens. When Sebastian and Ivy arrived, they could start to narrow down the best locations within the property for the ceremony, the dinner, the dance, the photos.

Later, in the days and weeks ahead, she could collaborate with Gabe on the perfect mix of the venue's traditional Christmas decor with the white-and-silver theme of the Jenkins-Davis wedding.

She eyed the magnificent staircase curving gracefully downward in an ever-widening arc. She could picture the bride and groom right there, the bride's train sweeping down over the stairs, the huge wedding party arranged on the steps around them. There would be thick garlands of pine boughs wrapped around the stone railings, softening them, and banks of white poinsettias flanking the stairs.

Or maybe not poinsettias, as the flowers were not her choice to make, she reminded herself. She was excited that in just three days she would be meeting with Hailey Thomas for the first time. Hailey was just as noted in her specialty of floral design as Alexandra was in hers of wedding planning, and she couldn't wait to work with her.

By December 14, Alexandra, Hailey and their combined teams would have transformed Parker and Parker from what it so obviously was—a slightly exotic rented venue—into a palace worthy of a fairy-tale beginning, and those magnificent oak doors at the top of the stairs would be thrown open to the invited guests of Ivy and Sebastian.

She glanced at her watch. She was a tiny bit early, and so she veered off the wide cobblestone path into the trees that flanked it. It was like entering a forest grotto in the middle of New York. And already, she could imagine silver and white Christmas trees, in the wedding theme colors, threaded into this little wood, turning it into an absolute enchantment.

She was about to turn and find the pathway again when a sound froze her in her tracks.

It was a child's giggle.

It was impossible. The wooded copse was empty. For a moment, Alexandra wondered if her mind had fabricated the giggle, just as how, when she slept, a child sometimes danced through her dreams.

She pulled herself together. Today was just not a good day to indulge the thoughts of a child who had almost been. Invariably, that what-if led to sadness, and Alexandra reminded herself sternly she was in the business of selling happiness.

Alexandra scanned the shrubbery and saw nothing. The giggle came again, breathless, muffled. A heap of raked leaves twitched suspiciously, and then she noticed a tiny black patent-leather shoe sticking out from under it.

She was relieved the bell-like laughter had not been a figment of her imagination, but still, something registered deep within her as being distinctly wrong.

It could be that she was interrupting a game of hide-and-seek, but where were the other players? And where was the adult supervisor?

There was no one else in this shaded area that she could discern. In fact, the silence was deep, given that all of New York hummed only a stone's throw away.

There was another muffled giggle and another tremble from under the pile of leaves.

Alexandra looked at her watch again. She was cutting it close. Still, she didn't feel right about leaving the child to her own devices in the Parker and Parker gardens. Despite the fact it felt like a private estate in the middle of the British countryside, the truth of the matter was they were practically at the center of New York City!

She edged closer to the pile of leaves. She had a wealth of experience with children, because her sister and brother had provided her with a half dozen rambunctious, lovable, energetic nieces and nephews.

That was her family. It was good enough. More than enough! It didn't fill her with longing for what might have been. It didn't!

"I haven't seen a pile of leaves like this in *forever*," Alexandra announced theatrically. "So, even though I am much too old, I'm going to jump in it. Here I go! One. Two—"

Before she counted to three, a small figure erupted from under the pile, squealing.

"No, no! Don't jump! You'll squish me!"

"My goodness!" Alexandra said, pretending to be startled. She took a step back. "A fairy!"

That was, indeed, what the small girl looked like. Leaves clung to a pink angora beret and a white cable-knit sweater, and a pink plaid skirt was stuck to bright pink tights.

But Alexandra realized it did not look like a fairy's face gazing at her—more like an angel's. The child's hair sprang in luxurious black curls out from under the beret. She had thick lashes, emerald-green eyes, plump cheeks and the most adorable bow of a mouth.

Alexandra had not done this for a long time: her baby would have been… She felt a shocking ache of longing, a stage she had thought she was long past. She quickly squashed it.

Not today.

The girl looked no more than four, and there was still no adult in sight.

"I'm not a fairy!" the child declared. "And you're not *that* old. I thought you might be a witch."

"Thanks," Alexandra said dryly. "But if you're

not a fairy, who are you? It seems to me only a fairy, not a small girl, would be out in the woods all by herself."

"I'm hiding from my nan," the girl said with mischievous glee. "And I'm good at it, too."

Alexandra tried not to let the alarm show in her face. "But how long have you been hiding? Your grandmother must be very worried about you."

The girl looked puzzled. "I'm not with my grandmother."

"Your nan?"

The child was silent.

"Your mother, then? Honestly, someone must be looking for you?"

The little girl blew out her lower lip and cast her gaze down at her feet. "I don't have a mother," she said sadly. "She died."

"Oh, I'm so sorry!"

The sad tone dissolved, and she lifted her chin to look at Alexandra appraisingly. "Would you like to be my mommy?"

There was a tricky question, loaded with all kinds of potential to cause both hurt and false hope.

"Well," Alexandra offered carefully, "of course, I'd love to be your mother. You look perfectly adorable. But you can't just pick up mothers in the woods on a whim."

"I don't know what a whim is, but I'd like a mother who would jump in leaves," the girl said.

"My daddy says I'm not 'dorable. I'm a perfect little monster."

"I'm sure he's teasing when he says that."

"Or maybe it's true," she offered carelessly, then tilted her head and smiled a small, charming smile. "Would you love to be my mommy if I was 'dorable *and* a monster?"

She was unusually articulate for her size. Precocious. It seemed there was going to be no correct answer for that question, so Alexandra felt it might be best to ignore it and address the more urgent matter at hand. Someone was looking for this mite, and probably desperately, too.

Alexandra firmly held out her hand. "Come on, we have to find your nan."

The tiny minx actually looked like she was considering darting the other way, but then, with a sigh of surrender, she took the proffered hand.

There was that *feeling* again, as Alexandra's hand closed around the warmth and sturdiness of the little girl's smaller one. She felt almost dizzy with longing.

This was ridiculous! She spent all kinds of time with her nieces and nephews and didn't feel as if she was being freshly immersed in grief, as she did now.

The child obviously knew her way around this tiny wood very well. She led Alexandra straight out and to the path.

A man's deep voice, edged in desperation, penetrated the silence of the woods. "Genevieve!"

The child giggled.

"That's you, isn't it?" Alexandra asked.

She nodded.

"It's not nice to frighten people," Alexandra said firmly. "It's quite naughty." They stepped out of the shade of the trees and onto the cobblestones.

A man was standing just outside the double oak doors at the top of the sweeping staircase that led into Parker and Parker, his gaze anxiously scanning the grounds. Even from a distance, and even though he was obviously agitated, it was apparent he was an attractive man.

A very attractive man.

He looked to be about midthirties and was dressed with the casual and utter sophistication that those comfortable with wealth were able to pull off: a dark gray sweater over a crisp white shirt and narrow-legged dark denims over boots.

He was tall, probably an inch or two over six feet, and beautifully proportioned, with wide shoulders, a broad chest and the flat stomach of the very fit. His legs, encased in those denims, were long and powerful-looking.

"Who is that?" Alexandra said on a breath. Obviously not *nan*!

"That's my daddy."

Of course. His hair was as black as the child's,

and for that matter, Alexandra's own hair. But it lacked his daughter's playful curls and was short and crisp.

The faintest hint of a shadow darkened the hollows of his cheeks, touched the slight cleft of his chin. He was extraordinarily handsome, and Alexandra wasn't sure if the pure potent effect of him was increased or decreased by a sternness in his features that made him seem quite formidable.

Though the little girl didn't seem to think there was anything formidable about the man at all. She let go of Alexandra's hand and skipped away. She turned back to stick out her tongue and then dismissed her and ran toward her father.

"Daddy! Daddy!" she cried. "I was lost."

Instant relief relaxed his features. He came down the stairs with the agility and speed of an athlete. He met the girl as she came up the pathway and swept her into his arms with ease. The look of gratitude on his handsome face was intense, and for a moment he didn't look quite so formidable.

"That lady found me," Genevieve said, pointing at Alexandra.

Alexandra felt grateful, given that stuck-out tongue moments ago, that the little minx had not proclaimed that she was a kidnapping victim, and Alexandra her abductor!

CHAPTER TWO

THEY CAME TOWARD her then, the child riding in the man's strong arms, her own arms wrapped around the gorgeous column of his throat.

Because of her growing success—a recent tabloid had called her Wedding Planner to the Stars—Alexandra increasingly found herself meeting the rich and the famous. She met celebrities, dignitaries, sports stars, entrepreneurs. A prince—Crown Prince Giovanni—was even going to be the best man for the Jenkins-Davis wedding.

She prided herself on the fact she was never intimidated by anyone.

And yet, as this man's shadow fell on her, and his green eyes—so like his daughter's, only minus the innocence—pinned her, she suddenly felt ridiculously tongue-tied, like a high school girl meeting her crush.

There was that renegade *longing* again.

But he was the kind of man who would create those kind of longings—for someone to hold on to, for someone to talk to deep into the night—in every female he encountered. He was one hundred percent confident in his masculinity, utterly breathtaking and stunningly gorgeous! And the ease with which he carried the small girl intensified the nearly magnetic pull of him.

But even as she drank in the tangy scent of him, she was aware of a kind of power radiating off him—a presence.

And there was nothing warm and fuzzy about it, despite the little girl who was so comfortable in his arms.

In fact, the man seemed very intimidating. Cool. Standoffish. Alexandra's original impression of sternness—of something faintly formidable about him—was underscored by his nearness.

Alexandra glanced at her watch. She was running late now. She was aware of feeling relieved that she had an appointment to get to. She didn't like these longings. She didn't like the fact that things she thought she had long laid to rest—or at least outrun—could be coaxed to the surface in a breath.

She didn't like feeling off balance in her well-ordered world.

"Hello," he said, his voice a gravelly scrape of pure sensuality that felt as if it was touching the back of Alexandra's neck. He freed a hand and extended it. "I'm Drew Parker."

"Of…of Parker and Parker?" she stammered. She *never* acted like a starstruck teenager. Not even when she was a teenager! So why was she suddenly reviewing her outfit—a perfectly professional black blazer, a sweater and slim black Klein trousers—critically? Why was she wishing for higher heels instead of ballet flats? Why was she wishing her hair was down, instead of scraped back into a respectable bun? She had to pull herself together.

Some shadow crossed briefly through the green of his eyes. "Yes," he said, jostling his daughter in his arms. "Here we are. Parker and Parker."

A different partnership was in that shadow that crossed his eyes, and Alexandra remembered the little girl's words.

I don't have a mother. She died.

"It's a pleasure to meet you, Mr. Parker."

"Drew, please."

Alexandra took his extended hand and it closed around hers, his grip hinting at tempered strength, and some terrifying awareness of him shivered through her whole being. She slid her hand back out of his, resisting an urge to look at it to see if it was smoking.

She had been burned by desire before and it had left her life in ashes. To feel it again now was a warning, not an invitation.

"What a beautiful place you own," she said in a rush so that he wouldn't know—or ever guess—what an impact his hand on hers had had on her.

"Ah," he said, turning and casting a rueful glance over the shoulder of the child at the building behind him. "It's much like owning a cat. You don't, really. It owns you. And it will tolerate you, barely, if the pampering is up to its rather exacting criteria."

It was such a delightful way of describing the old beauty behind him. It hinted that he wasn't just attractive, he was intelligent, which made him all the more intriguing. Still, his tone and his eyes remained cool and reminded Alexandra she had a busy, fulfilling life of her own.

That kind of intrigue she could live without, thank you very much.

"I'm Alexandra Harris," she said. Not a flicker of recognition crossed those handsome features. Of course, he owned the place. He probably didn't involve himself in the day-to-day operations of it.

"She said she would *love* to be my mommy," Genevieve announced.

A dark slash of an eyebrow—faintly accusing—was raised at Alexandra. She could feel her cheeks burning crimson.

"That's a bit out of context," she said.

"A contest!" Genevieve said breathlessly. "For a mommy!"

"You don't hold contests for a mommy," Drew said, a trifle wearily. He shot Alexandra a glance that somehow made the quest for mommy her fault.

"But it's a good idea!" Genevieve insisted, taking her father's cheeks between her two hands, and forcing his face toward her, to ensure his full attention. "She needs to jump in leaves. Bake cookies. Tell bedtime stories."

It was exactly the kind of mommy Alexandra had once thought she would be.

"I want an *alive* mommy."

And she had wanted an *alive* baby. Life could be so cruel.

The fact that he was fully aware of that vagaries of life appeared in the expression that crossed those handsome features. It made Alexandra's heart, already in a precarious position, feel as if it could break in two.

He was obviously a man who was successful and in control. A man who would give this small sprite anything she asked for.

Naturally, she had found the one thing that some tragedy had prevented him from giving her.

And if Alexandra was reading his expression correctly, it was the one thing Drew Parker had his heart set against giving his little girl.

An *alive* mommy.

He looked like a man who gave his heart once.

And forever.

Knowing that with a strange certainty filled Alexandra with an acute sense of failure. She had taken those forever vows once. And believed them with all her heart.

And yet, here she was, divorced.

She looked into his stern, closed features and wondered what he would think of that. And she also wondered what it would be like to be loved by someone so fierce in their commitment to love, to be the one who his face softened for…

Better, Alexandra warned herself, to keep this meeting with Drew Parker all business, as hard as that might be with Genevieve in his arms eyeing her with the avid interest of a child who desperately wanted to interview candidates for a mommy.

"Oh!" Alexandra said, looking at her watch. "I'm afraid I have an appointment. With Gabe Evans. Maybe you would be kind enough to point me in the direction of his office?"

"I'm sorry, Gabe isn't here today."

All those anxieties rushed up her spine. If catastrophe had a smell, Alexandra was pretty sure it was in the air right now.

"Not…not here?" she stammered.

"His mother has taken a turn for the worse. He's had to take a leave of absence."

Gabe hadn't even thought to call her? Still, if his mother had "taken a turn for the worse," that inferred some kind of long illness. It explained so much, really. The feeling she'd had that he was distracted. His near-whispered conversations. Perhaps he'd been working from home? Working around his sick mother?

"Oh, I'm so sorry to hear that." She forced herself

to remain calm. She congratulated herself on the even, professional tone of her voice. "Still, there are some things it is imperative I deal with today. Who will be coordinating events in Gabe's absence?"

A shriek interrupted her, and a young woman dressed in a yellow T-shirt, yoga pants and sneakers came around the side of the building, saw them and raced toward them.

"Mr. Parker, you found her. Genevieve, there you are! I nearly had a stroke."

So, this was the *nan* then. A nanny, not a grandmother. She looked like a wholesome young woman, nearly out of her mind with worry.

Which, at the moment, Alexandra could seriously relate to.

"I'm sorry, Mr. Parker," the young nanny said in a rush. "I really am. As I said to you when I reported her missing, I just ducked into the restroom for one second. Honestly. One. Second."

"She was on the phone with her boyfriend," Genevieve announced with grave pleasure.

Drew Parker's face darkened. Alexandra had the cowardly thought she was glad his wrath would not be directed at her.

"Miss Carmichael," he said, his voice icy, "you came highly recommended by the best nanny service in New York."

The young woman's bottom lip began to tremble.

"And you lost your charge? Because you were on your phone?"

"I wasn't *only* on my phone. I was in the restroom. I mean, I can't very well take her in there with me. But it won't happen again, Mr. Parker, I promise."

The young nanny looked so crestfallen, and the child looked just a little too pleased with herself.

Stay out of it, Alexandra warned herself. But, naturally, she couldn't.

"In fairness to Miss Carmichael, Genevieve was not lost. I found her *hiding* from her nan in the trees over there. Under a pile of leaves."

While Miss Carmichael gave her a glance loaded with gratitude, Genevieve gave Alexandra a look that clearly crossed her off the mommy candidate list.

"Did you?" Drew regarded Alexandra with cool thoughtfulness and then asked his daughter gravely, "Did you run away from Miss Carmichael while she was in the restroom?"

"I didn't mean to be bad," Genevieve said.

"No," her father responded, with a sigh that was equal parts affection and exasperation, "it seems to come quite naturally to you."

"Yes, it does," she agreed contritely. She laid her head on her father's shoulder and stuck her thumb in her mouth, suddenly—and deliberately, Alexandra suspected—more baby than articulate little girl.

"How about if you go have some ice cream with Miss Carmichael?" Drew said gently.

Genevieve popped back to life and scrambled out of her father's arms. "I'd like the pink-striped kind," she announced.

Stay out of it, Alexandra warned herself again. But naturally, she could not. "I don't think ice cream is a very appropriate consequence for running away from her nanny."

Genevieve lowered a brow at her. Drew looked at her, stunned. Obviously a man in his position was not used to receiving unsolicited advice from strangers, especially when there was faint reprimand in it.

"And what is your expertise on children, then?" he asked. "You have your own?"

"No," she admitted. "I'm not married."

Now, why had she inserted *that* particular detail?

"I'm divorced," she added, quickly, as if that would put up a much-needed barrier between her and a man who looked as if he would never consider breaking a vow, under any circumstances.

Drew cocked his head at her, but he looked so unimpressed it made her rush on, practically babbling.

"My brother has four kids and my sister has two. I'm sorry, I realize it doesn't really put me in a position to give advice."

"You're right. It probably doesn't," he said coolly. "Still, tell me, if you must, how your brother or sister might handle a situation like this one."

Alexandra thought this really would be a good

time to apologize for offering an opinion on something that was none of her business. On the other hand, even though he was the man least likely to inspire pity, he was going to have a hard go of it if he kept rewarding the little girl for being bad.

Maybe she could offer just a teensy bit of advice before she backed off from it.

"First of all," Alexandra said tentatively, "both my brother and sister would have an expectation that they would be able to make a phone call or use the restroom without having to look for runaway children afterward."

"I see. And if there was an incident of a runaway child?"

"Well, Shaun would not be above raising his voice."

Drew Parker winced at that.

"Because obviously you have to make it quite clear running away, at any time, is not okay, and that running away in the center of New York City is particularly unacceptable. My sister would probably remove a favorite cartoon from the agenda. For a week."

Drew still looked annoyed to be offered advice by a stranger, and he looked unimpressed with the strategies, too. And yet, after looking at Alexandra hard for a moment, he turned and regarded his daughter thoughtfully. "No *Molly Mood Ring*. For a week. Or forever, if you run away from Miss Carmichael again."

Miss Carmichael looked relieved to hear a future mentioned that had her in it. Genevieve was obviously way too accustomed to running the show with charm and guile. Her brows lowered mutinously. And yet, was she ever so faintly relieved to be having some of the responsibility for running that show removed from her? Because, despite that mutinous look, she did not throw herself on the ground and start screaming, as Alexandra's niece Macy, who was quite close to Genevieve's age, might have done.

She tossed her head. And glared at Alexandra. "I don't want you for my mommy anymore."

"I'm very sorry to hear that," Alexandra returned solemnly.

Genevieve took her nanny's hand and marched away, nose in the air.

"Now, Miss Harris—or is it Mrs.? I'm sorry, the etiquette of address after a divorce sometimes evades me."

Was he just aloof naturally, or was he judging her about the divorce?

"I've returned to my maiden name." There was an awful temptation to explain her whole history to him. A hasty college marriage because of an unexpected pregnancy, a union that could not survive tragedy. But she forced herself away from that insane need to excuse her divorce to someone she didn't even know and made herself smile carelessly. "So, yes, Miss, but Alexandra is fine."

"You're not, per chance, in the market for a nanny position?"

She wasn't sure if this was progress: having gone from annoying him to being offered a position.

"No," she said, and glanced down at herself wryly. "When I put this on this morning, I was thinking high-powered executive, not nanny, so I'll be sure and mark that down as a miss. Just to clarify, I'm definitely not someone who'd throw over their whole life for a nanny position, as honorable as I think that work is."

"Just for the record, I don't usually proposition strangers."

Her cheeks reddened.

So did his, ever so slightly. "That came out wrong. It wasn't meant as an insult to your professionalism, but you just do seem, um, wholesome…and good with children."

Wholesome? She was going home and dumping this whole outfit right in the trash. Not that there was anything wrong with wholesome, but around a man like this?

He cocked his head at her. "There's something about you that does suggest jumping in leaves, baking cookies, telling bedtime stories. Genevieve spotted it right away."

What kind of betrayal of self was it that Alexandra would have much preferred he find her sexy rather than wholesome?

And what kind of betrayal of self was it that

what he described felt just the tiniest bit attractive? To throw away all the stress and pressure in exchange for days jumping in leaves, baking cookies, reading stories?

The life she had once thought she would have... that she had willingly set aside her university education and career plans for.

Though, if she was completely honest with herself, wasn't part of the attraction of the unexpected job offer him? Drew Parker was so obviously in over his head on the single dad thing. It would be rewarding—not to mention fun—to help him navigate that path.

Why was she leaving *complicated* out of that assessment?

"I love my current career very much," she said, the firmness in her tone directed more at herself than at him. "And I think Miss Carmichael looks more than capable."

His look of genuine disappointment could cause the strongest woman to feel weak.

"Ah, well," Drew said, running a hand through the crisp darkness of his hair, and becoming all business once again, "please tell how we, at Parker and Parker, can assist you today. I'm sorry, Gabe didn't tell me you were coming. As I mentioned, his mother is very sick and has been for some time. He's been quite distracted of late."

She'd noticed.

"I'm here about the wedding," Alexandra said.

His mouth dropped open, then quickly snapped shut, tightening marginally, and his eyes narrowed. Any bond that they had just established dealing with his precocious daughter evaporated.

"The wedding?" he said. Was there something faintly dangerous in his tone, and in the spark in his eyes?

"We've confirmed a booking for the entire week leading up to December 14."

His eyes flew to her left hand, looking for an engagement ring. He thought she was getting married!

"I'm a wedding planner," she said hastily. Why did she care what he thought? She wanted this to be completely professional, that's why! "Ever After?"

He looked at her darkly, with absolutely no recognition.

"My client is Ivy Jenkins," she said, a bit desperately, not above throwing some names around. "She's marrying Sebastian Davis."

"I'm afraid there's been some mistake, Miss Harris."

She didn't miss the fact he had returned to formalities.

"We don't do weddings here."

Apparently he was completely unimpressed with her name dropping.

"Not ever. And we are not going to start now."

CHAPTER THREE

DREW WATCHED ALEXANDRA'S mouth fall open. Her eyes—dark, soft, lovely as a doe's—widened in shocked surprise.

To be honest, he was shocked himself. A wedding planner? The unsolicited parenting advice—he hoped she couldn't tell how welcome it had been—coupled with the outfit and the prim hair had made him reach the apparently erroneous conclusion she might be a suitable nanny. But if not that, the no-frills ensemble suggested a lawyer or an accountant.

A wedding planner? Somehow he would have pictured someone a little more flamboyant. Soft pastels and maybe some ruffles.

But, a voice whispered to him, Emily had not been those things, and her vision for Parker and Parker had been all about romance.

Drew gave himself a mental shake. Emily's vision, and how painful it was that it had never reached fruition for her, was the reason he would never hold a wedding here. He had to stand firm on that…despite Alexandra Harris's substantial appeal.

"But…but the invitations are printed," she stammered.

She really was a beautiful young woman, tall and willowy, delicate of feature. That mouth that had fallen open—but was now pressed firmly closed again—was exquisite, wide, plump, sensual. Her hair—thick, black, luxurious—was pinned up in that very prim bun that had led him down the nanny-for-hire road. For some reason, his fingers practically itched to let loose those pins.

Which made Drew feel as shocked as she looked.

It had been a long time since he had noticed… He shook it off. Losing Genevieve, and then finding her, had rattled him. He was well aware he could not withstand another loss. The beating of his heart was just beginning to return to normal. Those moments before she had been found had been a torment of what-ifs.

This woman had found his daughter. And he was deeply grateful, though not grateful enough to have a wedding hosted here. There had been some misunderstanding, obviously. He would figure out what it was and send her on her way.

The quicker the better, because there was a contradiction about Alexandra Harris that was intriguing. She had announced she was divorced with a certain bravery, as if she was revealing her worst failure to him.

Why? Traditional lives were no longer the norm. Many people were divorced, and for many reasons. It was hardly a failure. But if she felt it was, why had she chosen planning people's happily-ever-afters as her profession? Did she want to believe, despite her own disappointment? Or because of it?

Drew recognized he had been lucky to find a love that had felt as if it would last, but even so, his and Emily's relationship had hardly been traditional. They had decided they would get married after Genevieve had been born.

He regretted that now. That Em had died a month before the wedding she had longed for. Here.

It hardened his resolve, even as he tried to soften the blow.

"The invitations are printed but not mailed?" he asked. "That should make a change of venue relatively simple."

It darted across her face that a lie might be helpful here, and he had to admit he admired her for not giving in to that.

"Not sent," she said, "but reprinting isn't really an option. They were designed by Kimura."

He tilted his head at her to show the name meant nothing to him.

"She's a famous Japanese artist. Each invitation has a snowflake on it and is ever so slightly personalized. They were extraordinarily expensive, and they are bound to become collector's items."

"Items that are a mistake quite often end up even more valuable to collectors," he said.

Her face got a tight look on it. "You don't seem to understand. The wedding *has* to be here."

"*You* don't seem to understand. There will never be a wedding here."

"But why?" Alexandra asked, her eyes leaving his and looking at the building behind him with unveiled appreciation. "It's so perfect. It's as if it was made for weddings."

It had been made for weddings, actually. And one wedding in particular. Emily's excitement at the realization of their dream came back to him.

"It's highly personal," he said. "I won't get into it."

Her eyes came back to him. Something in them flashed. Strangely, it made him want to smile. She seemed as if she would be a worthy sparring partner. On the other hand, if they crossed swords, sparks were going to fly.

"I have a contract," she said. Her voice was even and firm, completely professional, and yet there was the slightest bit of panic being betrayed by the tremble of those lips.

"A contract?" he said.

What on earth had Gabe been up to?

"Yes, for the whole week preceding the December 14 wedding date."

"A week?"

"It would be impossible to put together everything for a wedding like this one in one day."

A wedding like this one.

It spoke volumes. It spoke of that one unforgettable day, a dream-come-true kind of day. He wanted to be cynical: a no-expense-spared kind of day.

But instead, a memory that he had locked away for a long time thrust its way forward.

He could see Emily feverishly planning, a notebook in front of her, her tongue caught between her teeth, her hair tucked behind her ear. As she had glanced up at him, she'd been alive with light and laughter, spinning her dreams into reality.

What had triggered that memory? Ah. Hadn't she said those very same words? Teasing him when he'd talked about her time commitment to *the* day?

It would be impossible to put together a wedding like this one in a day.

Drew couldn't do this. He couldn't allow someone else to realize Emily's dream. It felt like it would be the worst kind of betrayal.

"I don't have the contract with me," Alexandra said firmly, "but, of course, I can produce it. It is legally binding, but that's hardly the point. At this late date, I wouldn't be able to find another suitable venue for such a big event."

The week preceding December 14. The very time he and Genevieve were supposed to leave for the many amusements of California, his plan for a perfect Christmas this year, since he felt he had failed his daughter so miserably last year. What did he know about giving a four-year-old a happy Christmas?

He squinted at Alexandra. He'd bet, with her passel of unruly nieces and nephews, she would know. For some reason, it made him resent her.

"I have the deposit check right here in my purse."

"Ah," Drew said, "you haven't paid the deposit yet."

Her face went very white, and he was annoyed to find he felt for her. She had rescued Genevieve, after all, he told himself.

"There's been a mistake, obviously," he said reasonably. "I'll have to speak to Gabe about what happened. I can reimburse you, personally, for having to get the invitations reprinted with a new address on them."

"You don't seem to understand," she said, her voice low and husky in its fury. "It's too late for that. Ivy has her heart set on this venue."

With Ivy Jenkins's kind of money, she could have anything she set her heart on. It would never be too late. Still, he wanted to placate the wedding planner.

"Don't worry. I've got many, many connections," he assured her. "We'll be able to find you another venue."

He was not sure he wanted *we* to be any part

of his dealings with her. No, Gabe had somehow gotten them into this, and Gabe could get them out. But could he? His mother had been so sick for so long. Now it looked as if the end was near. Expecting him to look after this—or even explain it—seemed petty.

"There is no other venue quite like this one," she said, "and certainly not on such short notice."

He was right about sparks flying if they crossed swords. There was a light in her eyes that was very passionate.

He did not want to think about Miss Alexandra Harris and passion. At all. Again, his eyes went to her hair. Again, he could picture pins flying.

"It's not going to work," he said. "I'm sorry."

"I have a contract," she reminded him again.

"But you haven't paid a deposit," he reminded her again.

She sighed, obviously annoyed with going in this circle.

"It's a point of honor, Mr. Parker—" Somehow, that arrow hit. Being honorable was part of who he was, a value he wanted to instill in his daughter. "Not legal wrangling," she continued firmly. "Your representative signed a contract with me. I trusted that. I counted on that. Now my reputation is on the line."

Her vulnerability weakened him further. He wasn't going to be here, anyway. He'd be thousands of miles away. Did it really make any difference? That's probably what Gabe had thought. Why make such a big deal of this at her expense?

"They're coming here," she said. "Ivy and Sebastian."

"Today?"

She nodded.

"Call them and cancel. Until we work this out." He recognized he was already slipping a bit—that this was no longer the out-and-out no of a few minutes ago.

"It's too late," she whispered. She looked over his shoulder and closed her eyes, tight.

"They're early."

He turned to see whom she was looking at. Of course, he knew who Ivy Jenkins was. The heiress to CEO William Jenkins's billion-dollar business was walking toward them. Ivy did not look like the powerhouse she was. At only a little over five feet, her tininess, coupled with her black hair being cut so short, gave her the look of a woodland pixie. Drew had met her socially on a number of occasions.

But he hadn't put two and two together when Alexandra had mentioned Sebastian Davis. He recognized the younger brother of one of his own close acquaintances, Mark Davis.

Sebastian let go of Ivy's hand and came toward him, hand extended.

"Drew, so good to see you."

Drew slid a look to Alexandra. Hope was now fighting with the desperation in her lovely features. She hoped, because he knew Sebastian, he would change his mind.

"I can't thank you enough for allowing Ivy and me to have our wedding here," Sebastian said softly. "I know it must be painful for you. Mark didn't think you'd ever have a wedding here."

Mark—one of the many friends he had lost touch with—had been so right. Out of the corner of his eye, Drew saw Alexandra watching him, her hope for herself being overshadowed by curiosity. And something even more dangerous. Compassion.

Ivy came forward, took both his hands, bussed his cheeks and looked deeply at him. Any question about her prowess in the business world would be laid to rest by the intensity in her eyes.

"Sebastian told me how you and Emily had planned Parker and Parker together and how you thought yours would be the first wedding here. Clearly, I'm beyond honored that you would allow it to be us."

Despite their gratitude, Drew prepared to tell them it had been a mistake and there were going to be no weddings here after all. He hadn't woken up this morning expecting to be confronted with his deepest pain.

But, out of the corner of his eye, he could still see Alexandra watching him. Her new understanding was making her eyes even softer.

He did not want any more sympathy in his life in general, and he particularly did not want the sympathy of such a beautiful woman. Really, the look in her eyes made it more imperative to shut this thing down before it gained speed, like a runaway train.

But instead, he found her sympathy for him, despite his insensitivity to her predicament, touched some place in him that had not been touched for a long time.

Her career probably hung in the balance right now.

A mistake had been made that clearly was not her fault. And even though it was not her fault, the embarrassment it would cause her and the damage to her reputation and her business could be catastrophic.

Something whispered in him, *What would Em want me to do?*

Emily would expect him to be a man of honor.

That whispered inner voice also reminded him that he was a father now, raising a child that he hoped would be good and decent and kind. How could he have those kinds of expectations of Genevieve if he could not overcome his pain to be those things himself?

He pulled in a deep breath.

"Welcome to Parker and Parker," he heard himself say. "Let's have a look around, shall we?"

He dared to look at Alexandra. The light brightening her face felt like just about the most dangerous thing he had ever seen.

CHAPTER FOUR

ALEXANDRA WASN'T AWARE she had stopped breathing until she started again.

It would appear the wedding was on!

And yet her exhilaration at the bullet dodged was tempered by the pain she had seen in Drew Parker's face when Sebastian had revealed the real reason he was reluctant to have weddings here.

She saw the great effort it had caused him to overcome that pain. *For her.* Now he was leading the way into Parker and Parker, guiding a tour of the premises himself.

The building was beyond beautiful. The foyer was huge, with two staircases at the back of it on either side, curving up to the second floor. If she had thought the outside staircase lent itself to photos, this one was even more magnificent.

Ivy, one of the richest women in the world, who had seen everything there was to see, had tears sparkling in her eyes. This was one of the things Alexandra admired most about Ivy. Despite her wealth and all the perks of her upbringing, she was genuine and likable. Ivy consistently used her position of power and wealth to give others—especially small businesses and charities—a helping hand. She probably even would have handled the change of venue with grace.

But given the look on her face, Alexandra was so happy that she didn't have to.

"I couldn't even imagine something this beautiful," Ivy breathed. "I'd love a Christmas tree right here. A huge one. In our colors. Silver and white. What do you think, Sebastian?"

Sebastian obviously thought the sun rose and set by his bride. "I think that would be brilliant," he said.

This was one of the hardest things about coordinating a wedding for Alexandra. When the couples were a perfect match—which Ivy and Sebastian obviously were—something shimmered in the air between them that filled her with a longing that nearly took her breath away.

That longing was uncomfortably intensified today by Drew Parker standing so close to her.

But when she looked at him, his mouth was twisted into a cynical line. He raised an eyebrow at her, letting her know in a glance that he didn't like either the idea of the tree or the colors. But again, he saved her from embarrassment by not saying anything.

Alexandra forced herself into professional mode and slipped her notepad out of her purse.

"I'll take notes as we go. We're meeting in a few days with Hailey Thomas, so we can coordinate the floral design with other decor considerations then. Mr. Parker, you are welcome to join us, of course, as we'll be drawing up the initial plans and you might want some input. Our meeting is on October 4."

"At Hailey's workshop," Ivy said. "I can't wait to see it. She's so amazing!"

Mr. Parker looked like he would rather have toothpicks driven under his fingernails than join them for the floral consult.

Still, he was the model of a gracious host as they toured the facility together—the sumptuous banquet hall behind the staircase, the huge meeting room that could be converted to a chapel, the lovely suite above it that would be the ideal place for the wedding party to get ready and could provide a sanctuary to retreat to if the day's festivities proved tiring.

"My office," Drew said, waving his hand at a door that was marked with a gold plaque that read Private. "And my daughter's and my living quarters."

She hadn't realized he lived here. She thought it would be an absolutely fabulous place to live. Alexandra was a little perplexed by how much she would have liked a peek behind that Private sign. Only because, she told herself sternly, seeing how and where he lived would give her more understanding of Drew Parker.

And what do you need that for? an inner voice reprimanded her.

She forced herself to focus on the tour. The entire building was the most incredible blend of elegance, opulence and glamour. Despite herself, she wondered if his living quarters would reflect the same style.

In every room, Ivy was full of suggestions to go with the Christmas-themed wedding: she even wondered if they could make it snow in the ballroom!

Alexandra avoided Drew's gaze at that suggestion.

Though Ivy and Sebastian really didn't need to inspect the behind-the-scenes areas, like the huge commercial kitchen, they insisted. Ivy was bringing in her own team of chefs, so that was one less thing for Alexandra to worry about.

Ivy was hugging herself with excitement as they completed the tour at the front door, where it had started. "What would you think about a Christmas-themed merry-go-round on that lawn over there?"

"I'll make note," Alexandra said dutifully, "for our meeting with Hailey." She glanced at Drew. He didn't look very happy.

Finally, Drew and Alexandra said goodbye to the ecstatic couple.

"We'll see you in a few days," Ivy called. "I can't wait to meet Hailey."

"I'm going to have to beg off that meeting," Sebastian told his fiancée, throwing an arm around her shoulder and squeezing her with affectionate regret. "Gio's going to be here."

He sounded genuinely sorry that he was going to miss the flower planning. What a gem he was, Alexandra thought.

Ivy shook Drew's hand once more. "Drew, it was so nice to meet you. I hope to use your venue for many events from here on in. My bridesmaid, and good friend Autumn Jones is involved with a charity called Raise Your Voice. Have you heard of it?"

"I'm afraid not."

"Well, you will. I can see them holding extraordinary events here."

Alexandra turned to Drew once the couple had gone. "See?" she said. "Good things are coming from this already."

He was silent.

"I just love that even today, planning for her wedding, Ivy is still thinking about others."

Again, he was silent.

"Thank you for agreeing to hold the wedding here," Alexandra said quietly. "You saved me, really."

He lifted a shoulder.

"Parker and Parker is incredible," she said, hoping to erase the dark look from his face. "It's far more than I hoped for. I feel as if no detail has been overlooked. It is, of course, the perfect wedding venue."

He looked pained, so she didn't add she felt it was totally wasted on conventions and other totally nonromantic events.

"I'm so sorry for your loss," she said softly. "I didn't know."

She suspected he was a man who was rarely uncomfortable, but he looked uncomfortable now, as he shoved his hands into his pockets and rocked back on his heels.

"I understand perfectly why you didn't want to ever have a wedding here," Alexandra said. "I'm not sure why Gabe didn't just explain it to me when I was so persistent."

Drew's mouth—which was quite lovely—tilted up cynically at the corner. "You? Persistent? I can hardly picture it."

He was being sarcastic, but in light of the fact the wedding was bringing back the pain of his loss, perhaps that was understandable.

"Well, if he had told me," she insisted, "I might have managed to overcome that character defect."

"I doubt it," he said.

He hardly knew her. But since he was insisting

on seeing her in such a bad light, now might be the time to come clean on everything.

"I do have a bit of a confession to make," Alexandra said. "It wasn't strictly persistence. There was a small bribe involved."

"A bribe?" he asked, shocked. "Why am I getting this feeling I don't know Gabe at all?"

"Oh! It wasn't a money bribe. It was a funny little thing. After I called the first time, he looked up my company. It's on our website that Ever After had done the wedding for Priscilla Morrison."

He cocked his head at her.

"She's Webber Morrison's daughter."

"The jazz musician?"

"Yes. I promised Gabe an autographed picture."

"That was the bribe?"

She nodded.

"That's strange. It's an odd thing to risk your boss's wrath over, and he knew I wouldn't be happy about this. Plus, in all the years we've worked together, I've never once heard him listen to jazz. If you asked me, I would have said he was a '70s rock kind of guy. I'm beginning to feel like I don't know him at all."

"Anyway, if he had told me your history, I might have backed off."

He didn't look at all convinced. "*Might* being the operative word? Besides, Gabe—or at least the Gabe I thought I knew—would never discuss my personal life with anyone. He knows I'm a very private man."

"Which makes me appreciate what you've just done even more."

"Don't make the mistake of painting me as a knight in shining armor," Drew warned her sternly.

And yet, wasn't that exactly what he'd been when Ivy and Sebastian had arrived? Hadn't he put his own personal feelings aside to ride to her rescue?

But then, as if to prove all that had been a lapse he already regretted, he said, "There isn't going to be any merry-go-round. And no snow in the ballroom. It's all just a little too fluffy. Not to mention it would likely require structural changes to the room."

"Oh, but—"

"I'm not enthusiastic about a forty-foot silver-and-white tree in the front entrance, either. Doesn't that seem over-the-top to you? Grandiose?"

There was a temptation to argue the point, but maybe, given the concession he had already made to allow the wedding, she would save that for a different day.

"Everything is subject to change at this point," she told him soothingly. And really, right up until the wedding day, not that she needed to share that detail with him.

He was not soothed. His tone was very stern.

"You're walking a fine line here between a tasteful wedding and a carnival. There aren't going to be any carnivals at Parker and Parker."

Any thoughts she might have had about Drew Parker being her knight evaporated.

"Did someone say a carnival?" Genevieve squealed, coming out the front door of the building. "I love a carnival!"

Thankfully, Miss Carmichael was close on her heels this time.

"It looks like you have your hands full," Alexandra said, still stinging from his insult that she might create a carnival, "so I'll be on my way."

"Are we going to a carnival?" Genevieve demanded. Drew scooped her up with ease.

"No, no carnivals," he said, but he raised a skeptical eyebrow at Alexandra.

"It's my job to make sure everything is extraordinarily tasteful," she said tightly. "Hailey Thomas, the floral designer, is, by my estimation, one of the best in the world."

He looked unconvinced. "Perhaps you could drop by after your meeting with Ivy and the floral designer and we can go over your plan?"

Alexandra wasn't sure if she was pleased or distressed by that. She was going to have to make it clear she, not he, was in charge of this wedding. On the other hand, they were going to have to consult about many of the wedding details, and probably often.

Still, she took out her phone and looked at her calendar. "Would three o'clock work? On the fourth?"

"It would," he said without consulting his own calendar.

"Is that when the carnival is?" Genevieve demanded.

"No," he said. "But it seems to me you have a birthday party that day, don't you?"

Despite his prickliness, Alexandra couldn't help but smile that his parenting skills ran so far as practicing the art of distraction. Even though he was so cranky, she decided to help him out a bit.

"My niece Macy is having her birthday party that day, too. She's going to turn five."

"Does she have a party dress?"

"She's not really a dress kind of girl."

"Oh." Genevieve sighed. "Mine is like a rainbow. I want to show it to you. Daddy, can I show her right now?"

As much as Alexandra was dying to see the inside his private enclave, she decided to show Drew some mercy since he was obviously as uncomfortable with inviting her in as she was eager to be invited.

"I can't wait to see your dress," Alexandra said, "but not today. I'll be here the day of the party, and if you're here, you can show it to me before you leave."

Genevieve beamed at her, carnivals forgotten.

Instead of looking appreciative of her help in the distraction department, Drew was looking at her with mild annoyance, as if she was ingratiating herself into his family unwanted.

Still, she couldn't be ungracious. Drew Parker had done her an enormous favor. His heart wasn't as black as his expression was right now. She was sure of that!

"Thank you again. You saved my life today. I owe you one."

Alexandra put out her hand, and he shifted the child to his other arm and took it.

Something pure, electrical and sensual leaped between them. Did their touch linger just a little too long? Once again, Alexandra had to stop herself from inspecting her hand to see if smoke was coming off it.

A shiver went up and down her spine. Was he looking at her lips?

Of course he wasn't! Still, feeling wildly awkward, she scrabbled through her purse, found the check and handed it to him hastily.

"Until next time," she said, way too brightly. "Should we meet here on the steps?"

"I think there's a workshop here that day. My office might be best."

The office. The one that was marked private. How silly that she felt eager to see it, as if it would reveal clues about him that his expression did not.

Alexandra, thankfully, had three days to get her composure back. Still, she spent way too much time deciding what to wear. It had to be appropriate to meet with Ivy and Hailey, and it couldn't even have a hint of stodgy nanny for her meeting with Drew after. To add to the challenge, it also had to be appropriate for a child's birthday party, as she was going to her brother's immediately following the afternoon meeting.

She chose a simple but sleek black dress, matching tights and shoes that brought her five foot nine much closer to six feet. Even with the addition of two and a half inches to her height, thanks to the world's sexiest shoes, she'd still be looking up at Drew Parker, and that was a rare thing in her world.

As she regarded herself in the mirror, Alexandra decided her hair pinned up was just too uptight. She let it down and smiled at the effect. She congratulated herself on achieving the perfect look: professional and ever so subtly spicy.

It turned out she was particularly happy for the professional part of that equation, because Sebastian had decided to join them for the meeting with Hailey after all.

And he had stunned them all by bringing his college friend Gio with him. Alexandra knew, of course, that Crown Prince Giovanni of Adria was going to be Sebastian's best man, but she had not made the connection that he was the Gio that Sebastian had referred to the other day.

Once the initial faint discomfort of being in the

presence of a prince was put to rest—were they supposed to curtsy?—the meeting was phenomenal, the energy and ideas flying. Hailey, thankfully, was quite good at tempering Ivy's more outrageous ideas. She would say, "I *love* that. But might it work a little better if—"

Together, the five of them—the guys having quite a bit more to add than Alexandra ever would have guessed—had come up with an exquisite rough plan for the wedding decor: rich, stylish, tasteful and utterly, utterly gorgeous.

As always, she made quick rough sketches as the ideas flew, adjusting them as they evolved. When they finally were all in agreement, she put sheets of blueprint paper on one of Hailey's floral tables and, to the delight of the others, did a final sketch for each setting.

"You could have been an artist," Ivy said, studying the drawings with admiration.

Indeed, she could have been. That's what she had gone to college for, after all… But she shoved that broken dream away. Not today. It was not cutting into her elation today.

She wanted to carry this feeling all the way to her meeting with Drew. When a plan came together, it always felt like this: as if she was on fire with excitement. She loved her job!

She headed to Parker and Parker to run the plan by Drew. He *had* to like it.

She found her way to the office and was rewarded for getting her dress just right by the slight darkening of Drew's eyes as she arrived.

The office did not reveal as much about him as she might have hoped. It was, of course, very exclusive, and very much like the rest of the building, with rich furnishings, good paintings, subtle wall colors, aged hardwood floors. But the space was like an exquisitely decorated hotel room and did not reveal anything about Drew Parker's personality.

The office only made her long to look past the next door, the one she assumed led to his private living quarters—she could hear muffled giggles coming from behind it—but that door was firmly closed.

As, she could not help but notice, was his expression. His obviously expensive suit—pale gray, with a dark shirt and a slender aqua-colored necktie—reflected that he was all business today.

"I can't wait to show you what we've come up with for an initial plan," she said.

"Well," he said, his cynical tone like a needle piercing the balloon of her elation, "I hope it's not too much of a carnival."

CHAPTER FIVE

DREW IMMEDIATELY REGRETTED the tone he had taken. There was no need to be rude. On the other hand, a man had to have some defenses!

Alexandra Harris looked absolutely stunning today. She was wearing a simple, sophisticated black dress that she somehow elevated to extraordinarily sexy. The skirt ended midthigh, showing off the incredible length of her legs. She didn't need them—at all—but the shoes gave her added height and made her look willowy and jaw-droppingly gorgeous.

Drew was fairly certain that his assessment that she could have a successful career as a model would be no more welcomed than his suggestion of a career as a nanny.

To add to the subtle sensuality created by the dress and the shoes, her hair was down.

It cascaded past her shoulders in a long, silky waterfall of jet black. If he had to describe it, he would probably use the word *glorious*. It made his mouth go dry.

And speaking of mouths, hers was just about the most luscious he had ever seen. He had embarrassed them both by looking at it a little too long at their last meeting.

She was radiating light, he presumed because she was so excited about the plan for the wedding. He realized it reminded him of Emily's excitement for their wedding, and maybe that was why he had felt compelled to dim her light a little by making that stinging comment.

Alexandra faltered just slightly but then tossed that shining wave of hair over her shoulder and lifted her chin. Her eyes were sparking.

"It's not a carnival," she said firmly, and then added, her tone lighter, "In fact, it's been approved by royalty. Crown Prince Giovanni of Adria, an old college friend of Sebastian's, who will also be his best man, was at the meeting."

Drew had seen many pictures of the prince. He was an extraordinarily handsome man, and notoriously single. Was that why she looked so damned radiant? Because she'd met a prince?

And what was that he was feeling? Good grief! Not jealousy?

That was impossible. He barely knew Alexandra Harris. He certainly did not have any kind of designs on her.

Did the prince? How could he not, when she looked so stunning today?

"Did you enjoy meeting the prince?" he asked,

even though he had clearly instructed himself it was none of his business.

"Oh, sure." She said it so dismissively that he wanted to laugh out loud.

With relief.

She opened her satchel—the prince, as far as Drew could determine, completely forgotten—and pulled some papers from it. Sketches?

"I talked to Gabe," he told her. He ordered himself to stay put, but instead he got out of his chair, came around the desk and stood beside her. He told himself it was to see the sketches better. The scent of clean hair and subtle but exotic perfume tickled his nose.

"How's his mom?" She glanced up at him. The softness in her eyes felt like something that tore away at his carefully constructed barriers.

It told him a great deal about Alexandra that that would be her first question. Not how did this mix-up happen, or why had Gabe defied his boss, but how was his mother?

"He said she was having a good day. But he sounded sad and a bit overwhelmed. Still, I couldn't see *not* asking him how he'd managed to square it in his mind that it was okay to book a wedding without my knowledge."

"What did he say?"

"Genevieve and I are going to California for the latter part of December for Christmas. He actually thought I would never know."

"California?"

"Studios. Amusement parks. The beach. Warmth."

"Just the two of you?" she asked, those eyes still resting on his face, so soft a man could fall into them as if he had been a long way and a long time from comfort, and they were a featherbed.

"The two of us?" He didn't really get her question. "Speaking? Gabe and I?"

She cast him a look that clearly said men were complete idiots. "You and Genevieve. Going to California?"

"Yes, just the two of us."

"For Christmas?"

There was an odd look on her face. "What?"

"It's not really for me to say," she said, but she looked pained.

"No. I'd like to know what you think." Particularly given last year's disaster.

"Maybe it's just me, but Christmas needs snow. Not palm trees."

"The first one would have had palm trees," he said, and he could hear the defensiveness in his tone. "Besides, snow isn't exactly a recipe for a successful Christmas."

"Well, of course, it's not the whole recipe!"

"What is the whole recipe, then?" He hoped it was that simple. A recipe. And once he had it, he could just follow the instructions carefully and to the letter. He'd bet they would not lead him to Finnish Lapland, where he had taken Genevieve last year.

"I'm not the one to ask for a recipe for Christmas happiness," she said.

He glimpsed something in her eyes. Pain?

"But Christmas, for children especially, is family time," she said and smiled. Had he imagined the pain, then? She continued, "New York is magical at Christmas. The tree lighting at Rockefeller Center, skating at the Conservatory, sledding at Pilgrim Hill, seeing *The Nutcracker* performed onstage."

With every activity she listed, her tone became more wistful…but that underlying thread of pain was still there. As a man familiar with pain, he was certain of this.

Maybe it was the fact he detected some faint common ground of pain, because he found himself sharing something he normally would not have shared.

"Genevieve and I don't have family. Emily and I were both orphans. I think it was part of what made the bond between us so unbreakable. We found each other in a world where we had been alone."

He ordered himself to stop there, but he did not stop.

"When we found out Emily was pregnant, we were over the moon. Not just because of the baby, but because we were finally going to join that exclusive club called family."

Again, he ordered himself to stop. And again, he did not.

"I guess that's not meant to be for some people."

She looked quickly away from him, but not before he glimpsed the genuine concern in her eyes. He should have been furious with himself for telling her things that had earned her pity. And yet, that was not what he felt.

What he felt was not alone. Of course, he had Genevieve, but sometimes being a single dad with a four-year-old made him feel more alone, not less so.

He cleared his throat. He had gotten seriously off topic here.

"Anyway, getting back to Gabe, you were right. It was the bribe that tipped him over the edge."

"He told you that? That he risked your wrath for an autographed picture?" she said, following his lead back to safer ground, thank goodness.

"He didn't have to tell me. I could hear the jazz music playing in the background. I asked who it was. Can you guess?"

"Webber Morrison," she said softly.

"He said his mom loved Webber so much. She had followed his career since she was a young woman. She had all his albums. He said the music was bringing her great comfort. I think he almost mentioned the signed picture and then realized I didn't know about it. I didn't tell him I did."

"He risked your wrath for his sick mom," Alexandra said. How could a tone so tender feel as if it was going to yank your heart right out of your chest?

"That's what I'd like Genevieve to know about family," he said. "All the things I never knew. Family is somebody who has your back. Family is somebody who will risk anything to bring you happiness in your darkest moment."

She actually lifted her hand as if she might touch him. He stepped quickly away from her, and her hand dropped. She looked embarrassed.

He noticed her eyes were fringed with an abundance of thick, natural lashes, and they were truly amazing. Dark brown, flecked with gold. Richly layered, deeply textured.

"Please don't give up on love," she whispered.

Ah. He needed to remember this. For some reason she could see his soul. He did not like being so transparent.

"How can I?" he asked, his voice stripped of emotion. "I have my daughter. I want her to know love. I want her to feel it from me. The way I feel it from her."

"Why do I hear a *but*?" she asked.

He sucked in his breath. That's what transparency did. Alexandra saw things that were best kept hidden, that made him feel vulnerable. "But I also want to protect her from its pain."

"Oh, Drew," she said, and he heard the impossibility of what he wanted in her tone.

What was it about her that brought this out in him? Really? He was confiding to a near stranger. And he hated it.

"Let's see what you've brought," he said gruffly, needing to move away from the personal, and quickly. "Let's see the grand plans for the wedding."

She opened her folder and laid a large piece of paper on the desk in front of her. She had done a rough colored pencil sketch of the outside of Parker and Parker, transformed for the wedding.

"Your sketch is quite extraordinary."

"Thank you. I took art for a while, before..." Her voice drifted away, and he glanced at her. He realized he did not have a monopoly on suffering.

"Before what?"

"Oh..." She lifted a slender shoulder. "You know. Life."

He did know. Life.

All of it—sharing his vulnerability with her, the quickly shuttered pain in her eyes, the unexpected beauty of the drawing—were evoking feelings in Drew to the point it felt as if his throat was closing. Where was all this coming from today?

He was suddenly acutely aware of the danger

of connecting with her, with a person who could pull such deep feeling from him.

Instead, he forced himself to focus on the drawing in front of him. Parker and Parker had been transformed into a vision worthy of a fairy tale. Not just any vision, but a Christmas vision. He did not trust himself to speak. She cast him an anxious look, and he just nodded.

She placed the next drawing in front of him, her shoulder brushing against his when she did so.

Was it partly his awareness of her that made her vision for the front foyer so electrifying? Again, the transformation was complete. The space was always magnificent, and yet the addition of trees and garlands, candles and wreaths, took it beyond beautiful. It was a wonderland of whimsy and wishes. It invited you to do what he least wanted to do right now—to feel something.

To feel the most dangerous thing of all. Hope.

"Did the prince do this?" he asked, and his tone had a deliberate edge to it. "It's all very castle in a fairy tale."

"Of course Gio had input—"

Gio?

"But, no, Hailey, Ivy and I came up with most of this. Do you like it?"

He found he couldn't speak. *Like* did not seem strong enough. It was exquisite. It was also the perfect setting for a wedding, what every single woman would hope for on her special day.

He just nodded. "It's okay," he said gruffly.

One by one, she laid out her drawings, her vision. It was becoming clearer and clearer to him that Alexandra planned weddings all the time. Though she had given the other women credit, he had already seen what Ivy's taste ran to. And Hailey's specialty was flowers.

Which meant Alexandra had largely created the *feeling* that was coming across in each of these sketches.

Hope.

What every wedding, at its core, was about. Hope. A hope that love was real and lasting. A hope that dreams could come true. A hope that, in the face of plenty of evidence to the contrary, love could make life better than it had ever been before.

Alexandra probably created this feeling, wove this magic, into every single wedding she did, even when the backdrop was far less spectacular, even when the budget was less extravagant.

Drew wondered if she had any idea what these drawings said about her.

She believed in something. She hoped for something.

Don't give up on love, she had whispered to him.

The last drawing showed the main ballroom in two stages: dinner, and then the tables cleared away for dancing.

It was like a magic wand had been waved and

the ballroom had become an enchanted forest on a winter's night.

"Are the trees real?" he asked.

"Yes." She glanced at him. He was glad she seemed uncertain how to read him now. "The plans call for thirty of them for the ballroom alone. Forty total. Fraser fir."

"That's a lot of needles to clean up," he said.

"You'll never know they were there," she promised, but he could tell she was hurt by his lack of approval. "Besides, everything is subject to change, right up until the day of the wedding."

"And you're able to create this illusion of a starlit night?"

"I have an excellent team of experts I work with all the time. What we do is a bit like creating a set. So, yes, it's very doable."

"Is it going to snow?" he asked. "Inside?"

That was hardly his vehement *no to snow* of a few days ago. So clearly, without even trying, she was weaving him into this enchantment of hers. He had to stop it. He had to pull back from it instead of leaning toward it.

She smiled. That smile did not make leaning back from her magic any easier.

"I hope it's going to snow. If you'll allow it. You can actually get fake snow. We thought we'd mix it with silver glitter and release it from hidden compartments in the ceiling during the last dance."

She hugged herself with excitement. "Every

single person dusted with the magic of the day before they leave."

He was being dusted with her magic right now.

"Of course, I'll take full responsibility for having it cleaned up, just like with the trees."

He could not trust himself to speak as he stared at her rendering and thought of people being dusted with the magic of love.

She frowned at his silence. "Are the plans okay, then?"

Okay? They were better than okay. He could see that this vision, this wedding being held at Parker and Parker, was so right.

It wasn't, as he had feared for so long, a betrayal of Emily to have a wedding here. It was, in fact, the exact opposite.

It was—particularly the way this was laid out—a way of honoring Em. Her belief in romance. Her belief in dreams. Her belief in love.

It was as if this was the part of his healing that he had been missing. That he hadn't even known he needed.

An *accident* had brought him to this. A mistake in bookings. This all would have been a secret from him if Gabe had not stepped aside.

He was a man who had lost the love of his life.

A tragedy like that did not lend itself to a belief in a larger plan. And yet, in this moment, he felt oddly illuminated.

And terribly vulnerable.

"Drew?"

He pressed his fingers to his nose and pinched the bridge of it.

"What's wrong?" she asked softly, her eyes on his face filled with concern. Not for her plan, but for *him*.

He pulled himself together. "Nothing's wrong," he said, keeping his voice carefully neutral, stripping all the emotion out of it.

She was still looking into his eyes. It was making him feel weak when he wanted to be strong.

She looked away from him, back at her drawings, something faintly pensive in her look now. He felt as if he started breathing again. She was obviously disappointed by his faint praise.

"So?" she asked, her tone brisk. "You're okay with everything? Not too much of a carnival?"

"I'm not sold on the snow. If you could rethink that…" he forced himself to say. "And it's too many trees. There are probably fire regulations."

"These are just the initial plans, ever changing at this point," she said, her tone clipped with hurt. "The details will come into focus as we go, and I'll need to check with you as they do."

He began to roll up the sheets of paper one by one.

Check with him? Over the details? It made his head ache, thinking of being around her—trying to keep his defenses up like this was exhausting.

"It's an ambitious plan," he said. "Yes, please

do check in with me from time to time. Though hopefully Gabe will be back soon and you can check in with him."

He handed the papers back to her.

"You'll probably be dealing mostly with him," he said.

Her mouth closed. She knew he was dismissing her. Good Lord. She probably had a prince floundering at her feet. Why did she look so distressed that their brief relationship was ending?

For that matter, why did he feel distressed about it?

She was dangerous to him. She was dangerous to his heart. She was opening doors that were better left closed.

"Goodbye, Miss Harris," he said firmly.

CHAPTER SIX

GOODBYE, MISS HARRIS?

Alexandra was stunned. She was really having trouble reading Drew Parker. He didn't seem enthusiastic about any part of her plan. Fire regulations? Rethink the snow, as if that wasn't the best part of the whole plan?

Why did she want his approval so badly? Why did she want his confidence in her ability to pull off the wedding of the century?

"You'll have to be involved," she told him curtly. "Obviously, you've just made it clear I can't just go ahead and plan without consulting you. It's your venue, and I'm not into the surprise of a last-minute veto on your part."

"There's no need to say that as if I'd be unreasonable when I feel I've been very reasonable."

"The snow and trees?" she snapped.

"Oh, that. Why don't you make a few tweaks, and you can text or email me changes and plans as they occur? Please feel free to stay in touch as much as you need to."

She considered the formality of the way he was addressing her. He was definitely trying to put distance between them. It felt as if they had gotten beyond that, somehow, when he had admitted he wanted his daughter both to know love and be protected from it.

It had felt as if a bond had been forged between them when he had trusted her with his vulnerability, his single dad doubts. She had even considered the possibility that, eventually, she would trust him with hers.

Now, *eventually* was no longer on the table.

Well, what had she thought? That he was going to help her every step of the way? That they were going to meet regularly to go over details of the wedding?

That, as they got to know each other, she was going to rescue him and his adorable daughter from a lonely Christmas?

Really, who was she to give any kind of advice around Christmas—to insist it was a family time—when she had distracted herself with work and had avoided her own family on the days leading up to Christmas for years now?

It wasn't that she didn't love doing the things she had mentioned to him with her nieces and nephews, sledding and skating and going to Rockefeller Center, but doing those things also filled her with a bittersweet longing for what might have been.

And as the days counted down to Christmas, the grief that people insisted time would heal seemed as undiluted as that horrible day a decade ago, when her worst nightmare had unfolded.

Alexandra shook it off. And with it she shook off hope.

Because, hadn't she hoped, in that moment when he had shared about Emily with her, that something powerful had passed between them, that maybe Drew was going to ask her out for dinner?

Hadn't she hoped she might screw up the nerve to ask him out for dinner if he didn't?

She glanced at his face. It was completely closed. His expression was cold. She shoved the rolled plans back into her bag. It was more than evident they would not be going for dinner together.

It was more than evident whatever connection they'd had was over. When Gabe came back, Drew was going to pass on dealing with her to him. And he was clearly hoping Gabe would be back sooner rather than later.

And then he would take Genevieve to California. Chances were he wouldn't even be here for the wedding. How could he not want to see these sketches brought, step by meticulous step, to life? How could he not want to see the flimsy stuff that dreams were made of become the strongly woven fabric of reality?

How silly to feel bereft about that, as if in Drew Parker she had caught a glimpse of a world more enticing than the one she had created on these papers, and the door to that world was being slammed in her face.

She, of all people, should know better than to hope. She turned to go. She did not want to risk shaking hands with him again. She hoped he might say—

"Wait!"

But, of course, it was not him. The door between his living quarters and the office had been flung open. Genevieve catapulted through, wearing the most delightful party dress, fit for a princess with its layers of multicolored ruffles.

"You weren't going to leave without seeing my dress, were you?" she cried, doing a pirouette in front of Alexandra. "I wanted you to see my dress. Do you like it?"

"It's absolutely beautiful."

"Look, my tights glitter."

"Yes, they do," Alexandra said. Her feeling of being bereft deepened as she thought of never seeing Genevieve again. Why such a deep reaction to the loss of such a short acquaintance?

It was better this way. If she could feel so attached—to both this child and her father—after such a short time, what would it be like if she got to know them better and then things didn't work out?

And one thing about being a wedding planner—you had an unfortunate front-row seat to things not working out.

Sometimes the couples didn't even make it to the wedding day.

And other times that couple who had been so in love, who had gazed at each other so adoringly, who had vowed, in front of the world, to stay together until death, didn't make it, either.

Alexandra always felt so sad when she heard of one of *her* couples not making it. She still even felt sad if the bride came to her to plan a second wedding. Once it had even been a third one. Though she tried her hardest, the magic of the first time refused to be recreated.

Of course, her first and only time had not been magic. Ever since she was a teenager, she had longed to have the perfect wedding one day. A surprise pregnancy had changed all that, and she'd had a hurried exchange of vows in front of a justice of the peace.

With a man who cared about her but who did not love her.

And whom she had tried so hard to love, but…

Alexandra shook it off. You would really think she would have the good sense to be cynical by now, to genuinely be glad Drew had dismissed her in the face of that elusive *something* leaping up between them.

"And this is the gift I got Brenna," Genevieve

said, not noticing Alexandra inching toward the door. She showed her a very badly wrapped box, and Alexandra cast the nanny, Miss Carmichael, a smile for letting Genevieve wrap it herself. But she frowned at the look on the nanny's face. She looked stricken as she gazed at her small charge.

"It's a Bonnie doll," Genevieve said, unaware of the look her nanny was giving her.

Alexandra stopped inching toward the door and looked again at the nanny, who was obviously screwing up her courage to tell Drew something.

Or was that Mr. Parker now? Since she was Miss Harris to him?

"Do you think she'll like it?"

"Of course she will," Alexandra said, though she was distracted. The only girl child in the universe not enraptured with a Bonnie doll was her own niece, Macy, who was going through a cowboy phase. Her party was Western themed.

Alexandra glanced at her watch. She really needed to go and felt grateful she had a place to go to where she wouldn't or couldn't wallow in her sense of loss.

Goodbye, Miss Harris.

Miss Carmichael was leaning into Drew. "I'm just leaving for the day. Um…"

"Is there a problem?" he asked.

"Well, yes, actually. I didn't want to be the one to tell her," Miss Carmichael said, and then she leaned even closer to him and whispered something in his ear.

He listened carefully and then straightened. He blew out his breath and then rocked back on his heels.

"So, I'll be going then," Miss Carmichael said with loud cheer. She turned and practically bolted out the door. Alexandra wanted to follow her, but there was something about the pained look Drew cast her that made her hesitate.

As she watched, he took a deep breath and crouched down in front of his daughter.

Good grief! What would give him that look, like a soldier about to inform a general of a failed mission?

"I'm afraid I have some bad news."

The child froze and turned slowly to look at her father.

"What?" she whispered, her eyes wide on his face.

He cleared his throat. "The party has been canceled. Brenna is sick."

Genevieve looked at him in silent disbelief. And then her face crumpled. And then the wrapped doll box fell from her hand.

"Noooo!" she wailed. She cast herself on the floor and began to beat it with her small fists and feet.

Drew scooped her up and held her tight. "I'm

sorry, pumpkin. She'll have it as soon as she gets better."

That was little consolation to Genevieve. She howled with fresh pain. Her tears ran down Drew's neck.

Drew cast Alexandra a look over Genevieve's head. It was such a look of universal longing: every parent just wanting to make the world right for his child, to take away moments of pain, to smooth over things going wrong.

It made Alexandra feel a foolish longing to do all the same things.

For him.

Or maybe it was really for herself. To delay the goodbye to this man and his child for one more brief period in time, even though logically she knew how unwise it was to do so.

Sometimes, the heart simply would not be overruled. Or maybe, this year, she was looking for a bigger Christmas distraction than ever.

And so, before she could think it through properly, or stop herself, she called loudly, over the heartbreaking wailing of the child, "I know where there's a birthday party."

Genevieve stopped howling with comical abruptness, as if a radio had been shut off. Two identical sets of green eyes fastened on her, Genevieve's hopeful, while her father looked more cautious.

It occurred to Alexandra she really should have

taken him aside privately. Now she had really put him in an impossible position if he wanted to say no.

Of course he wanted to say no! That's why he had just said goodbye to her with such finality. He didn't want to spend more time with her.

Still, she had jumped in now. Alexandra tried to tell herself it was strictly for Genevieve's sake, and not to draw out her relationship with her father.

So, she went on bravely, "It's my niece Macy's birthday today. I was just on my way there. You are welcome to join me."

Drew, to her everlasting relief, did not look at all as if he felt she had backed him into a corner. Despite the fact he wanted to distance himself from her—hand her off to Gabe as soon as possible—he looked at her now like he was a drowning man and she had thrown him the life preserver. He looked at her with the heartfelt relief of a man who loved his child unconditionally.

"Are you sure?" he asked. "You don't need to check that it's okay to bring extras?"

He was certainly a different person when his daughter's happiness was at stake! It made her heart melt.

She actually laughed. "Last I heard the entire preschool class was going, her cousins, her sister and her two brothers. And probably whoever they want to bring." She couldn't resist teasing him a tiny bit. "It *will* be a regular carnival."

"Oh!" Genevieve said. "Daddy! I told you I love carnivals!" And then she scrambled down out of his arms and turned a joyous circle, laughing merrily.

Then he laughed, too.

Alexandra had not seen Drew laugh yet. In fact, she had barely seen him crack a smile. She was sadly aware of what a rare event it must be when Genevieve stopped midcircle and looked at her father with astounded delight.

His laughter chased some shadow from his eyes and lifted some weight from his shoulders. It also made him—in a flash of brilliant white teeth—possibly the most attractive man Alexandra had ever laid eyes on.

"Let's go then," he said, and Genevieve squealed her delight. "Shall I call a car?"

"I was just going to take the subway," Alexandra said. "We're going to the Flushing neighborhood in Queens."

"The subway!" Genevieve said. "Can we go on the subway, Daddy, please?"

"I hate to say it," Alexandra said, because of course riding in any car he called would probably be a luxury, "but at this time of day, the subway might be faster."

And so they ended up walking to the subway

station with Genevieve skipping between them, holding both their hands.

Alexandra could not help but notice that in New York, the city where people made a point of not noticing each other, the little girl, her party dress peeking out from under her parka, attracted indulgent smiles.

And so did she and Drew. Of course, people would be assuming Alexandra and Drew—Drew holding the badly wrapped birthday present— were mommy and daddy, and that they were a perfect little family unit. It was a fantasy that was very hard not to enjoy.

Riding the subway was such a simple thing. Alexandra had probably done it hundreds—if not thousands—of times, and yet, today, experiencing it with Genevieve's wonder made her so aware of every little thing, not the least of which was Drew's shoulder pressed against hers as he held his daughter on his lap.

Her brother lived in a middle-class section of New York, not the kind of neighborhood or house Manhattan people like Drew Parker or Ivy Jenkins would be familiar with, and as they got off the subway, Alexandra had a moment's doubt.

What was she doing?

This wasn't Drew Parker's world. This was working-class New York. What if Genevieve— children being children—blurted out something about where her brother lived that hurt everyone's feelings?

They came to her brother's block. It looked a touch shabby to Alexandra now, even though she had grown up in this neighborhood and still lived in an apartment around the corner from here. Despite the breathtaking expense of the real estate, this was still where the plumbers and electricians and secretaries and shop clerks lived. For the most part, this was not where the moguls and millionaires were.

She was aware that the yard was a shambles of toys and bicycles, the paint was peeling, and the front porch was leaning as if it might fall off. The Christmas lights from last year had not been taken down, and one string of them hung drunkenly off the peak of the roof.

And she was suddenly aware of Drew's suit, the dark knee-length cashmere coat he'd thrown over it, the expense of the plaid wool scarf knotted so casually at his neck.

What had she been thinking, bringing a millionaire here?

Genevieve stopped and looked at the house for a long time. And then she turned to Drew. Alexandra held her breath. Maybe they would decide not to even go in.

"Daddy," Genevieve said, her tone reverent and excited. "Look. It's a *real* house."

"It is," Drew said, and he shot Alexandra a

smile so loaded with gratitude she thought she might melt.

She had the awful thought that maybe it was she who had become the snob!

Party noises were already spilling from the house, and the laughter called to them like a lighthouse that would beckon sailors who had been lost at sea.

"Give me the present," Genevieve said excitedly, as if it were her entry pass to the festivities.

It was utter chaos inside. Alexandra cast a worried look at Genevieve. She was an only child. How was she going to handle this? But Genevieve was not shrinking behind her father's leg, at all. She looked enchanted.

"Auntie!"

Alexandra bent over to give her niece Ashley a hug. "These are my friends, Genevieve and her father, Mr. Parker."

"Drew is fine," he said.

"Genevieve, I love your dress," Ashley said. "And your tights are the best. Sparkly!"

Genevieve preened at the approval of someone just enough older than herself to really count.

"Is that a present for Macy? Let's go put it in the present pile." Ashley held out her hand, and without so much as a backward glance at her daddy, Genevieve went with her.

Alexandra's sister-in-law, Shelley, made her way through the crowd of rambunctious children.

As a mother of four, she looked slightly frayed, as always, but so at home in all this happy chaos that Alexandra felt that familiar stab of longing.

Alexandra introduced her to Drew. Her eyes went back and forth between Alexandra and Drew with such embarrassing hope that she *finally* had a boyfriend that Alexandra felt compelled to speak up.

"Drew and I are working on a wedding together."

"But you aren't even engaged yet!" Shelley said. She was so pleased with how hilarious she found herself that she didn't appear to notice the sudden awkwardness between Alexandra and Drew.

CHAPTER SEVEN

ALEXANDRA FELT DREW shift his weight uncomfortably beside her. She gave her sister-in-law a warning look.

"We're business associates," she said sternly, trying to stop any further shenanigans from Shelley.

But Shelly did not look chastised in the least. Instead, she cocked her head at Drew and studied him with avid interest.

"Somehow," she decided, "you don't look like someone involved in the wedding business."

Alexandra slid him a glance and couldn't help but notice he looked insultingly pleased by that assessment.

"I'm not involved in the wedding business. Genevieve, unfortunately, had a party canceled this afternoon," Drew said. "At the point when she was on the floor screaming like someone being murdered, Alexandra obviously saw I was in over my head and took pity on me. She rescued me, so thank you for having us on such short notice."

"I thought it would be a shame to let such a beautiful party dress go to waste," Alexandra said, trying to head Shelley off. It didn't work.

"But how did you happen to be together?" Shelley asked, with way too much interest.

"I own a venue Alexandra is using for an upcoming wedding."

"Oh? Which venue?"

"Parker and Parker," he said.

"Oh! I love that building. So enchanting!" Shelley shot Alexandra a look. She might as well have had a blinking neon banner running across her forehead that said *keeper*.

"Thank you," Drew said with genuine pleasure.

"It looks just like a mansion. Have you ever considered having a Halloween event there?"

"I haven't," he said.

Shelley rolled her eyes. "As Genevieve gets older, you will see Halloween is *the* second most important event on the junior calendar."

"And the first?" he asked.

Shelley looked at him closely. "Are you a single dad?"

Alexandra realized that she might not have thought through this part of inviting Genevieve to her niece's party—the inevitable interrogation of showing up at a family event with a man.

He nodded.

"A single dad," Shelley said with a sigh, as though this status made Drew more irresistible than the crown prince of Adria. She shot another look at Alexandra. The blinking *keeper* banner was stronger now.

"What made it obvious?" he asked.

"Oh, first that *you* were dealing with a child screaming on the floor. That's usually pretty solidly in the mommy department. And also that you had to ask what the first important event on the junior calendar is. So, for future reference, this is what you need to know. Any child divides up their year by events, and how importantly they rate them. Christmas is number one."

Alexandra noticed he frowned at that.

"Followed by Halloween. Then their birthday—not their brothers' or sisters' birthdays—theirs."

"Genevieve is an only child."

"Oh, dear," her sister-in-law murmured.

"Oh, dear?" he prodded her for her meaning.

"Well, it's just that that comes with its own set of problems, along with the——" Shelley finally caught the fact Alexandra was glaring at her, and didn't, thank goodness, finish her sentence where she was going to give poor Drew a complex about the set of problems that his child was going to endure as a result of being raised by a single dad.

"Anyway," Shelley finished a bit lamely, "*the* list in order of importance—Christmas, Halloween, birthday, summer vacation, Easter, spring break."

Alexandra was not unaware her sister-in-law shot her an accusing look when she mentioned the importance of Christmas to her children. She wasn't going to be made to feel guilty. She did lots of things with her nieces and nephews around Christmas. It's just as it came nearer, she withdrew.

"Should I take notes?" Drew asked. His brief frown at the mention of Christmas again—at the head of the list—had disappeared, and his voice held only smooth good humor.

He was being very good-natured about the whole thing, which Shelley would probably take as an invitation to keep questioning him.

Thankfully, Alexandra was spotted by four more of her nieces and nephews, and they were swarmed. She had to comment on each one's party finery, and she received sticky kisses and long hugs.

She finally pulled herself from the heap of children.

"This is my friend Drew," Alexandra said. She placed her hands affectionately on the head of each child as they were introduced, Shelley's remaining children, Colin and Michael, and her sister Heather's girls, Adelle and Catherine.

She had always felt you could tell a great deal about a person from how they were around children. She loved how solemnly Drew greeted each child, and said their name, and how he offered his hand, and didn't even try and wipe it surreptitiously on his pants after he got a sticky handshake.

"I want to show you my new skates," Michael said.

"And I built a fort," Colin said. "It's in my room. Can you—"

"Not now," Shelley said firmly. "Off with all of you. I think we're about to begin decorating cupcakes in the kitchen."

The children stampeded off at the mention of cupcakes.

"Is Heather here?" Alexandra asked. If she had thought Shelley's interrogation of Drew was invasive enough, it would be nothing compared to what her sister, Heather, was capable of.

Obviously, she really had not thought this through. And what would happen when her brother, Shaun, showed up? He'd be grilling Drew mercilessly, and then the whole gang of them would be getting ready to post banns at the church.

"Heather had the good sense to drop off the kids and leave," Shelley said. "It's going to be chaos here and we're bursting at the seams. If you're okay leaving Genevieve, and unless you're wild about decorating cupcakes, why don't you two go grab a nice quiet drink somewhere and come back in a while?"

Alexandra was aghast at how obvious Shelley was being.

Shelley turned away as if it was already decided.

"Maybe I should just tell Genevieve," Drew said uncertainly.

"Never mind that, it'll be an hour before she notices you're gone," Shelley said with the ease of someone who dealt with children all the time. "I'll tell her when I see her. I can always text Alexandra if there's any problems."

The noise and chaos seemed to fade away. Alexandra was aware of Drew watching her, faint amusement upturning his mouth.

He pushed open the door behind him.

"Shall we?" he said.

Alexandra was distressed to find she felt as tongue-tied as a teenager on her first date as she stepped back out the door into the crisp fall air.

Drew took in a deep breath of the fall-scented air, trying to center himself.

He had known when he saw Alexandra's drawings today that she hoped for *something*. He had tried, almost desperately, to distance himself from that. And yet, here he was.

Seeing her, so much a part of that family, those children swarming her adoringly, the light that had come on in her face as she bestowed kisses and dispensed hugs, had solidified exactly what it was she hoped for.

And deserved.

A family.

Of course, he was the man least likely to give that to anyone. He didn't even know what it was. He and Emily had had that in common.

And still, they had hoped.

He could not have such a hope crush him again. But what about Genevieve? It was what he wanted for her, wasn't it?

For her to be part of something? To belong? To have hope?

"Do you know where to go?" In light of his thoughts, what was he really asking? Did Alexandra have the road map for life?

"This is my neighborhood."

This was *her* neighborhood. Children. Family.

"There's a cute, quiet place around the corner."

They were talking about places to go for a drink, nothing more. Except she seemed to sense something more.

"You seem pensive," Alexandra said, a reminder it would be very hard to have secrets from a woman like her.

"Do I?" he hedged. "I guess I'm just thinking of all the things I don't know about raising a child. I don't even know how to give her a good Christmas, and apparently, that's the most important one of all."

"Here it is."

It was a small brick building with a sign over

the door. He read it out loud. "Tequila Rocking-bird?" Despite himself, he laughed. "It's clever. What's a Rockingbird?"

"Their specialty drink," she said in a whisper. "Created, I think, to make the name work. Don't try it."

He opened the door for her. Such a simple thing, holding open the door for a woman.

But when she brushed by him, it filled him with a longing he had not allowed himself to feel for quite some time.

A longing to not be quite so alone with it all.

That was a longing that had been exacerbated by the visit to that delightfully chaotic party. By her sister-in-law, knowing, with such ease, all the rules for raising children, how it all went, how it all was supposed to go.

The pub was tiny, nearly empty and cozy with its rabbit warren of cubbyholes and eclectic furniture. Alexandra knew her way around it, because she led him to a little enclave at the back. They sat at coffee table by a stone fireplace. She took a love seat, and he took the deeply distressed leather chair across from her.

"We have a special," the waitress told them when she arrived. "Our very own Rockingbird cocktail."

Alexandra cast him a look and ordered a glass of the house white. He liked that. There was something very unpretentious about it.

He would have normally ordered a scotch, even though he didn't really like scotch, not even the much-touted Glenfiddich he would usually ask for. Now that choice seemed pretentious, even though not liking it would keep him sipping slowly, or barely touching it. One thing about being around a woman like this one? You did not want to drink too much.

You did not want to let your guard down at all.

So, what devil inside him made him order the Rockingbird?

He looked at her. She raised an amused eyebrow as if to say, *I tried to warn you.*

Everything about her seemed like a warning. The light from that flickering fire illuminated her, and though she had looked radiant when he'd first seen her today, when she was brimming over with plans and excitement, now that radiance had deepened, as if she had pulled all that love from her nieces and nephews inside her, and she was lit from within.

He realized his guard was already down. Her scent, already familiar to him, wrapped around him. Her foot accidentally brushed his under the table, and it felt as if an electric shock went up and down his leg. She felt something, too, because she withdrew her foot rapidly.

"Sorry," she said, her cheeks coloring, and making her look even more beautiful in the warm glow of the fire.

Though he felt like he had seen her true beauty as those children swarmed her.

The drinks arrived. She took a satisfied sip of her wine. He took a taste of the Rockingbird.

"Well?" she asked.

"It's shockingly good."

"Uh-huh. That's tequila. It's the Samson and Delilah of drinks. Careful, it's hiding a pair of scissors in its pretty dress."

That was also love, he thought. And it was a good reminder to be wary of the charms of this beautiful woman.

"You seem pensive again."

He had hoped for small talk. He had assumed Alexandra would be good at small talk. He supposed she met all kinds of people—including, he reminded himself a little sourly, princes. He had hoped she would guide the conversation easily and they would talk about safe things like music and movies, maybe the weather. Perhaps they would touch lightly on politics.

But, oh, no, here he was contemplating love's daggers, not that he intended to let her know that, charms of the Rockingbird notwithstanding.

"Just mulling over all the things your sister-in-law made me so aware I don't know," he admitted. "I'm dreading Christmas."

It felt like a confession, not really much better than love's daggers as a nice, light conversation.

She cocked her head at him.

"I made a mess of it last year."

"In what way?"

"I took Genevieve to Finland."

"What?"

"Obviously, when she was two, Christmas was no problem. She was hardly aware of what Christmas was. But last year was different. I wanted it to be spectacular. Memorable."

Being around people like Shelley made him aware of what he had really wanted. To not feel so alone with it all. To somehow capture the *feeling* of it. In this he had failed miserably.

"So, I took her to a real, live Christmas village."

"There's such a place?"

"Finnish Lapland."

"It sounds perfectly lovely," she said dubiously. "What was wrong?"

"Besides everything? We had jet lag. There was a sauna in our cottage. It burped a little steam at her and she decided monsters lived there. The Northern Lights confirmed her suspicion we were in a deeply strange place. Then, Santa didn't *look* right. Or sound right. The reindeer smelled, and there was no Rudolph. You cannot even imagine how cold it was as we took our sleigh ride across the Arctic Circle. To add to that, she told Santa what gift she wanted, but it was a secret from me, so guess what?"

"Wrong toy," Alexandra said. Her eyes were so warm, so full of tenderness and sympathy.

"So wrong."

What had happened to his drink? He hadn't had the whole thing, had he? That was impossible. Still, there seemed to be a fresh one there. He put it to his lips. It felt like he was drinking a spell. No, a curse that was making him talk too much, reveal too much.

"And this year, California," she said, that same annoying, dubious tone in her voice.

"The amusement parks have Christmas themes," he said defensively. "They're famous for them!"

"Ah."

Alexandra didn't ask him why he wasn't going to stay here. There was no reason to tell her. None.

"Emily loved Christmas," he heard himself tell her, and took another deep drink from his Rockingbird.

CHAPTER EIGHT

"I THINK," DREW CONTINUED, despite ordering himself to stop—both talking and drinking the drink, "Christmas may have been the only thing Emily loved better than a wedding."

"Ivy said yours was supposed to be the first wedding at Parker and Parker."

"It was," he said. His words didn't seem slurred. Not at all. It felt as if they were rising from some place deep inside him. Trying to stop them was like trying to stop bubbles rising in champagne. Impossible.

"The whole thing—Parker and Parker—was her idea, start to finish. She was in love with love. She radiated love. And she wanted to create this perfect, magical place for couples to begin, for them to dedicate their lives to each other."

"She succeeded," Alexandra said quietly.

"We actually bought it and started the renovations before she got pregnant. That was an incredible surprise, because she'd been told she couldn't have children. I wanted to get married before the baby was born, but she was desperate to have the wedding there—the first one in Parker and Parker—and she wanted it to be perfect. The renovations went longer than she'd anticipated, so she insisted we reschedule the date."

He heard his voice crack ever so slightly and took another drink. Just to lubricate his throat.

"She died when Genevieve was two months old, one month before our wedding."

"I'm so sorry."

"Part of the reason we bought Parker and Parker," he said, "was she wanted Christmas there. Our first Christmas there—our only one, as it turned out—we had just taken possession. We'd spent all our money. We didn't have any furniture or any decorations. She was pregnant, and we lay in front of the fire on a stone floor wrapped in a blanket and she dreamed out loud. Of decorating the building for next year. Of December brides. Of hosting Christmas parties for homeless kids."

Enough! He looked at the drink accusingly. Well, it wasn't as if Alexandra hadn't warned him.

"She dreamed," he said, and heard his voice crack again, despite his efforts to lubricate it, "of our first Christmas with our baby. That's why I can't be there. I just can't."

"I understand," she said, and he looked at her and knew that she did.

"That's why, as much as possible, I haven't

been involved in the hands-on running of Parker and Parker. Thankfully, I still have my career, just for those moments that being a single dad doesn't keep me fully occupied."

As he said it, Drew was deeply aware how he had filled every moment trying to outrun pain, trying to protect his daughter from pain.

Alexandra cocked her head at him, an invitation to talk more, though he knew he had talked quite enough.

"I'm an architectural engineer, which is every bit as dull as it sounds. When we found the building, it had been abandoned for some time. It needed a lot of work. Recreating it as a venue was the perfect melding of our different strengths, but after the refurbishment, I considered my job done. I could never take over the making-dreams-come-true part."

Was he babbling? If there was one person who was not a babbler, it was him. Not that anyone would know it at the moment. He ordered himself to be silent. And then kept talking.

"And what kind of dad can I be to Genevieve when I can't be the making-dreams-come-true type? Last Christmas being a case in point."

There it was. His deepest insecurity laid out shamelessly before Alexandra.

"You're doing a great job with Genevieve," Alexandra said, and there was something so firm in her voice, he wanted to believe her.

"Really?" He heard the cynicism in his tone.

"Of course!"

She was just trying to make him feel good.

"What about the Christmas fiasco?"

"Life is full of fiascos. Your job isn't to give Genevieve a perfect life, it's to give her the tools to cope when life is not perfect."

"Your first meeting with her," he reminded Alexandra, "she was running away from her nanny. Who was, by the way, the seventh or eighth one I've had. That's hardly an A-plus on the parenting report card."

"There are no A-pluses on the parenting report card. Ask Shelley. Or my sister, Heather. You've raised a very confident little girl. Given the number of nannies, it really speaks to you that Genevieve feels so safe and secure in an ever-changing world."

He regarded her thoughtfully. It occurred to him she was being genuine.

Still, it was hard to accept the compliment. "Maybe if she was a little less confident—some might call it naughty—we'd be able to keep a nanny."

"I doubt that," Alexandra said. "I doubt it's Genevieve at all. Look at the nanny you have now. She's at that age—marriage, college, travel. Life calls."

He had never once seen a nanny leaving as anything but his own fault for having such a headstrong daughter, and he was surprised by how grateful he felt to see it in this new light. "Thank you," he said. It shouldn't have meant quite so much to him, but it did.

As they talked, it became very apparent to Drew that Alexandra was smart, sophisticated and successful. And utterly gorgeous. And also deep, sensitive, compassionate, talented, with a dash of wise added to the whole picture.

And yet...single. And for some reason, that didn't seem right to him. He was shocked by how badly he wanted to know her at a different level, at a deeper level, and shocked by how the Rockingbird seemed to have erased his own boundaries and made him ready to push against hers.

"Why aren't you an artist, covered from head to toe in paint and surrounded by a million children of your own?" he blurted.

She raised an eyebrow at him. "What makes you think the life I have isn't perfectly satisfying?"

"I think it is perfectly satisfying. But not wildly exuberant."

"Who has a wildly exuberant life?" she asked him, a bit defensively.

This was going wrong. He was being too personal. He needed to leave it alone. It was certainly too soon in their relationship for this.

Their relationship? They did not have a relationship!

And so, he was shocked when he could not leave it alone. "What is in this drink?"

"About three ounces of tequila," she said.

"And a little black magic," he muttered.

"Possibly," she said, and that beautiful mouth quirked upward.

He wondered what her mouth would taste like. Tasting it might be the perfect thing to shut him up.

But since he couldn't very well just lean across the table and kiss her, he just kept on talking.

"When I saw your sketches today, and then saw you with all those children, it felt as if I was seeing what your dreams are made of.

"I'm sorry," he said when she looked stunned by his way-too-personal observation.

"The life you have is not always the one you dreamed of," she said.

So she didn't have a wildly exuberant life? Or she didn't have the one she had dreamed of?

She blushed, as if she had revealed way too much about herself, which maybe she had.

"And now I'm sorry," Alexandra said. "I don't really have to tell you that."

"I want to know about the life you dreamed of," he said softly.

She hesitated. And then she took a sip of her wine and looked at him appraisingly.

Drew was aware he was holding his breath. She was trying to decide whether to trust him with something deeper of herself, something that she was acknowledging he had already guessed.

To be honest, he did not know if he was worthy, and at the same time felt as if he would be crushed if she found him unworthy.

"I was going to be an artist," she said. "Or at least have a world that had something to do with art. Ever since I was small, I was that dreamy kid with the sketch pad. Drawing was as natural to me as breathing. A few pencil lines could become a butterfly, or the cat sleeping in the flower box. I didn't have to labor over it. I could do a sketch in minutes.

"When I was a teenager, I was obsessed with castles and princesses, but by the time I was going to college, I had put that aside—publicly, at least—and considered myself quite the serious artist."

"And what were you drawing privately?" he asked her.

She took a sip of her drink and looked at him, again, deciding.

"Brides, weddings, flower arrangements. I was hiding my secret romantic self from the very serious world I was entering."

Warning, his mind screamed, *she has a secret romantic self. Run!* But he didn't run.

"And then what happened?" Drew heard himself encouraging her softly.

Alexandra had not expected this conversation to take a turn like this or for him to ask her to be so transparent. Nor had she expected to *want* to tell Drew her secrets. But he had told her some of his, and there was an intensity building between them that demanded honesty. That demanded, somehow, she leave the polite conventions behind and bring her complete self to him.

"What happened?" she said. "I met a boy. Isn't that always what happens? I was at college, living away from home for the first time. I was learning exciting new things and trying on exciting new ideas, and I felt so grown-up and independent. I was basically bedazzled by life.

"He was in my art class, and we were both just brimming over with fresh ideas and discovery, and the discovery extended to each other.

"Only once. But guess what? Once was enough." Her voice cracked. She had never really told this story, start to finish, to anyone. Why start with him?

Because his extraordinary green eyes had darkened to moss. Because he was watching her so intently. Because he was a man a woman wanted to give everything of herself to. Her successes. Her failures.

Her deepest secrets.

"I was pregnant. And terrified. But he was excited. He knew what to do—said we'd give that baby a mommy and a daddy. We'd make a family. He'd get a job. I'd get a job up until the baby was born. We could return to school later. We didn't have any money, but in this kind of blur of fast decisions, I found myself quitting college and getting a job. I found myself at city hall saying *I do* to an almost complete stranger."

"How was your family with all this?"

"It was a shock, at first, of course. My brother, Shaun, wanted to kill Brian, as if he'd made that baby all by himself. But pretty soon everyone saw how eager he was to do the right thing by me and the baby, and they welcomed him in. You've seen my family. Controlled chaos. There is always room for one more. Everybody in my whole family believes a baby is always a blessing. They celebrate life, no matter what it throws at them."

"That's pretty amazing," he said. "What everyone wants in a family. A great backdrop for happily-ever-after. So, what happened?"

"We lost the baby."

"I'm so sorry," he said, and his voice was pure gravel. "I should have known that. When I first met you, I asked about children. I'm glad you have your family."

But that was where the love of her family got complicated. They didn't really understand, after the loss, her need to hold that grief to herself. They couldn't understand how everything they had—the babies, the homes, the laughter, the chaos—made her so acutely aware of a baby with perfect fingers. And perfect toes. And one shock of golden hair. Who had never drawn a single breath.

She realized she had started to tremble. He realized it, too. He came around the table, unhesitatingly, and sat on the love seat beside her. His hand covered hers. His scent—clean, masculine, spicy—was reassuring in a way she couldn't quite understand.

"It was a stillbirth," she told Drew. She hadn't expected to cry. Not after all this time, but she did.

As if it was the most natural thing in the world, he put his arms around her, drew her into his chest. His hand found her hair and stroked it. It felt as if it were a homecoming. It felt as if he was pulling more words out of her. They spilled out of her mouth and onto his chest, right above his heart.

"Brian and I didn't have anything in common beyond that baby," she choked out. "And art. It wasn't enough. Our shared grief held us together for a bit, but then his brush with captivity made him long for freedom, and so when that door opened, he leaped through it. We were divorced before we'd even been married a year."

She didn't tell him they still talked once a year. On an anniversary of sorts, and not their wedding anniversary, a day that was completely forgettable. No, they talked on that sad day that they had lost the baby. No matter where he was on the planet, when the clock struck midnight on that mid-December day, as the rest of the world was entering, in earnest, the happiest season of all, her phone rang.

She pulled away from Drew's chest and found a beautiful, pristine white square of linen pressed into her hand. She dabbed at her eyes and gave him a watery smile.

See? I'm pulling myself together.

"When I quit college, I went to work for a company that catered events. I couldn't go back to school. I was too changed. Over the years, the business evolved into a full planning service that did weddings. When my boss decided to retire, she split off the wedding planning part of the company and sold it to me. And so here I am, giving the beautiful wedding—and the happily-ever-after—I never had to everyone else."

CHAPTER NINE

ALEXANDRA WONDERED IF she had ever said that out loud before. It felt as if she had just blurted out her deepest secret.

She looked into the deep green of Drew's eyes and realized the danger of starting to believe in those kinds of dreams ever again.

Those kinds of dreams just ended in disillusionment and brokenness if you allowed them to see the light of day. But he already knew the price of believing in dreams. Their shared pain leaped between them, a bond.

She had gotten the tears under control, but she was still trembling.

But she realized the trembling wasn't from her memories now. It was from an awareness of how close he was, an awareness that a perilous electricity was shimmering in the air between them.

She put her hand on his chest, not to push him away, but to feel the beat of his heart beneath her fingertips, and then to guide herself in closer. She leaned toward him.

He did not seem surprised.

No, it was as if he had been waiting for this. As if this moment was inevitable between them. She lifted her chin and touched his lips with her own.

That destructive force that she had been trying so hard to hold at bay—hope—crashed in around her like the sea waves exploding over rocks.

His lips carried the sharp tang of tequila. They were soft and the furthest thing from soft at the same time.

Alexandra was sure she had only had half a glass of wine, and yet the taste of his lips made her feel utterly intoxicated, as if she was swan-diving into a star-studded black night and had no idea where she would land when she finished dropping through the darkness.

She felt weak in a way that made her welcome weakness, even though she knew that the world required her to be strong.

His hands tangled in her hair, and he claimed her mouth completely. And she let him. She welcomed him.

And as their encounter deepened, she was so aware this was not the clumsy, driven passion of youth. As much as it was spontaneous, it was also a conscious choice between two adults.

The kiss was mature, like spirits aged in an oak cask, rich and deep with a hint of darkness. It was exhilarating, and she rose to it, her every nerve end singing.

It penetrated her awareness that her phone was announcing an incoming call. She didn't care. It could wait.

Except, annoyingly, the sound penetrated the deliciously altered state she was in, like an alarm bell stridently announcing danger. Didn't that distinctive *boing, boing, boing* belong to someone?

Someone important?

She drew herself away from his kiss.

"Shelley," she announced out loud, and saw the instant fear of a man who had lost everything once already cross his face.

Alexandra wrenched herself completely away from Drew and pawed through her bag for the phone.

She put it on speaker. "Shelley? Is everything okay?"

"There's just a little problem at the party."

"Is Genevieve all right?" Drew asked, despite Shelley's relaxed tone. He went from seductive kisser to protective daddy in the blink of an eye, and there was something extraordinarily compelling about that transformation.

"Oh, yeah, nothing urgent. No blood, hysterics, tears or bruises. But Genevieve has retreated to the upstairs linen closet. She would like her daddy to come get her now." Shelley's tone was amused rather than concerned.

"What brought that on?" Alexandra asked, worried.

"Apparently Macy told her she doesn't like Bonnie dolls. A catastrophe in a four-year-old's world."

"Tell her Daddy is on the way," Drew said.

He got up, dropped some bills on the table and reached for her jacket and helped her slip it on before he put on his own. That gesture made her aware there was no point in offering to pay her share.

His smile was self-deprecating. "So much for the confident little girl who feels safe and secure in the world," he said.

"You're way too hard on yourself about this parenting gig."

"Easy for you to say. It's not your kid crying in the closet." He started humming. "It's my party and I'll cry if I want to…"

She smiled at him, and they went out into the crisp night. Somehow everything seemed more vibrant than it had before they had gone into the pub. Before he had kissed her.

She felt like a princess, awaking from a long sleep. The autumn night seemed alive. The air tingled in her nose and throat and lungs. Leaves, enchantingly outlined in gold under the streetlights, shivered on their branches.

"She's four," Alexandra said, "and I assume she's not used to being around a ton of people. She wants her daddy. You're what makes her world safe and secure."

He looked at her, and she saw she had managed to validate him in an area where he felt insecure. He looked like the kind of man—confident, successful, in charge—who was probably very unaccustomed to insecurity in his world. Being a daddy had humbled him.

His hand closed around hers, and the feeling of the night being alive intensified as they walked through it hand in hand.

Also intensified was Alexandra's awareness that a man like this could set back the recovery of a wounded heart.

Could she enjoy this moment and not ask for others? Maybe she should enjoy this moment all the more for knowing she would have to let go of this man after tonight.

Of course, they would still have to discuss some details about Ivy and Sebastian's wedding. Of course, she would still have to confer with him.

But the dreams that had been let loose with that kiss—all her wild need, and her desire so long bottled up, so long seen for what it was, disruptive and dangerous—needed to be put back in their vessel.

Before it was too late. Before they passed the point of no return.

She slipped her hand from his as they approached the house. There was no need to add to the complexity of this with family conjecture, since she had already decided it must end before it started.

Really, it was akin to stamping out a little tiny spark before it was allowed to become something else.

A single spark of passion had ruined Alexandra's whole life once already, burned it to the ground. She, of all people, should know the danger of playing with fire. And there was no denying it was fire she had felt when she had invited Drew's lips to her own.

By the time they arrived at the house, Genevieve had emerged from the closet. In fact, she danced to the door, her face alight as Drew walked in.

"Look, Daddy, I have a Bonnie doll."

Genevieve looked like a different child to the one who had been dropped off. Her sparkly tights had a rip in them, and her dress was crumpled and had a cake stain on it. Her hair was also a mess under a princess party hat.

Though her cheeks had tear streaks on them, she looked all better now. Still, in retrospect, Alexandra thought, she might not have been quite ready for this rambunctious crew.

Not that that was her call to make! She had better be very careful before playing mommy without an invitation.

Did she want that invitation?

"So I see," Drew said, his lips twitching, thankfully with amusement and not horror. "How did you happen to get a Bonnie doll?"

"I gave it to her."

"This is my niece Macy," Alexandra said, scooping her cowboy outfit–clad niece up into her arms and kissing her plump cheek. "Macy, this is Drew. He's Genevieve's daddy."

"She was in the closet," Macy reported. "So I went and got her. I told her she could have the doll if she came out."

"That was very nice," Drew told her.

"Not really. I don't like dolls."

Macy was apparently impervious to the fact that her rejecting the gift might have driven poor Genevieve into the closet in the first place. For someone who had been contemplating the role of mommy just moments ago, this was one of those times where it was a relief to be an auntie. Shelley could deal with the etiquette of rejected gifts.

Or maybe she had—maybe that was why the peace offering in the closet had been made. And it had worked, too.

"Macy's my best friend now," Genevieve announced solemnly. "We're coming here for trick or treat, aren't we, Macy?"

Macy scrambled down out of her aunt's arms. "Yup," she cried.

Shelley came across the living room. She looked nearly as disheveled as Genevieve.

"Yes, please come," she said. "It's a block party.

So much fun. Everybody dresses up. Adults and kids. I think they've booked some kind of spooky bouncy tent."

"A spooky bouncy tent," Genevieve breathed excitedly. "Daddy, we'll come, won't we?"

He hesitated. His eyes found Alexandra's. In them, she saw the same struggle she was experiencing.

Did they let this spark find the life it was looking for, or did they squash it out, firmly, before it took hold?

But there were larger questions.

To be open to life, or not?

Looking into the depth of his eyes, other questions rushed at her. To be open to the unexpected? To be fully alive, instead of just going through the motions?

She had lost that baby such a long time ago. How long was she going to protect herself from pain? How long was she going to live in fear of making a mistake? How long was she going to be controlled by the past?

Maybe it had been too long already.

"It might be nice to come to a party I didn't plan," she said tentatively.

"Are we going to come, Daddy?"

Drew didn't look at Genevieve. He looked at her. Long and hard, his gaze opening a world of possibility that had been completely closed to her.

"We would love to come," he said.

Suddenly, Alexandra felt frightened. What was she doing? She was so rarely impulsive, and she reminded herself that she almost always regretted it when she was.

On the other hand, she had weeks to think about this. To back out. There was no reason he and Genevieve couldn't come without her.

Though she knew they wouldn't.

When had she become this person? So eager to protect her heart, she would keep a little girl—one who had lost her mother—from knowing the joy of community? Of family?

"I would love to come too," Alexandra said.

But if it was about Genevieve, if she was being as altruistic as she wanted to be, why was she already thinking of her costume?

She already knew it wasn't going to be Little Bo Peep or Little Red Riding Hood or any of the things anyone would expect of her.

Drew sat in the deep, luxurious leather rear seat of the car he had called. The company knew him, and so they had sent a car with a child seat. Genevieve, new doll clutched against her, had fallen asleep almost as soon as she had been strapped in.

Her hair was matted and stuck to her forehead and her cheek. Her dress was wrinkled and stained. The little stocking had a rip in it. A funny little smile played across her slack, chocolate-stained mouth.

He remembered her declaration that the house they were visiting was a *real* house.

And that's what she looked like right now. A *real* little girl. The observation stung.

He turned his thoughts away from his failings as a parent, to the woman who had said he was too hard on himself. He'd offered to drop Alexandra somewhere, but she had said no, she lived just around the corner.

It must have shown in his face that he didn't want her walking home alone, because she had laughed and said she would stay at the party until her brother got home, and then he would insist on walking her to her place.

One kiss.

And Drew was feeling protective of her.

One kiss.

And he felt restless.

One kiss.

And he felt hungry for more.

One kiss.

And he felt helpless to say no to that party invitation. But was it really the party invitation—and his daughter's excitement about it—that he'd been helpless to say no to?

Or was it the chance to see Alexandra again?

He would put it all from his mind. His biggest responsibility, of course, was Genevieve. His business kept him occupied. Last time they had spoken, Gabe had said that Drew should begin to think about replacing him. It looked as if it was going to be a long haul with his mother, but now Drew realized he welcomed the extra duties to fill up his days. He told himself, firmly, that putting that kiss from his mind was going to be the easiest thing he had ever done.

The car pulled up in front of Parker and Parker. Drew carefully undid the harness of the car seat and hefted his sleeping daughter in his arms.

She nestled against him, a puddle of warmth, boneless. She barely shifted as he made his way, carrying her inside. Genevieve was trusting him completely. To put her needs first. Always.

And what did that mean in terms of that kiss with Alexandra?

Drew realized, irritated, he had managed to put that kiss—the one that was going to be the easiest thing ever for him to forget about—from his mind for all of thirty seconds.

CHAPTER TEN

ON THE DAY of the Halloween block party, Drew stared at himself in the mirror, aghast. He was aware it was possible for a man to push a kiss to the back of his mind, just as he had vowed to do. And yet, still, here he was, being confronted with how that kiss had changed him, regardless of how successful he had been at not thinking about it.

Maybe it shouldn't be as surprising as it was that the—white-hot—meeting of lips had altered him. Heat melted things, after all. But what it seemed to be melting was some barrier around his heart.

He'd sensed it when he started calling Gabe every day, not just to discuss business, but to find out how he was doing. How his mom was doing. He'd sent dinner over for them, twice. He'd also found a rare Webber Morrison session online and sent Gabe the link.

But now the proof of some new and uncomfortable softness confronted him in the mirror.

Naturally, Genevieve had told Miss Carmichael about her new best friend, the *real* house and the invitation to the party.

Miss Carmichael had come to him and offered, shyly, to take care of their costumes, as she helped with costumes for an amateur theater group. She said she could borrow some things and make others.

This was one of the changes to his heart: he saw her differently. In a gentler light than he had before. As a whole person, with a life outside his household. He noticed how young she was. He noticed she'd been crying. It didn't take much prodding of Genevieve to find out there had been a breakup with the boyfriend.

And still, she wanted to make them costumes.

Before the kiss, he wouldn't have noticed a kind of bravery in that. And to be honest, it had been a relief to hand over the whole costume question to someone else, so it was helpful to both of them.

Genevieve was totally enraptured with the whole idea of Halloween. She was no longer a baby, content, as she had been last year, to be stuffed into a coat with bunny ears and taken around to the apartments of a few friends.

No, this year Halloween was taking on a production-like ambience. Genevieve and Miss Carmichael had decided on a Bobo Robbins theme. This was a surprise, as Drew had thought Genevieve would lean more toward princesses.

However, Bobo was a cowboy cartoon character—Macy's favorite, apparently—who had a faithful dog, Chance, and a talking owl, Cowly, who rode on his shoulder.

Drew, thankfully, hadn't had to give costume selection another thought. He'd been grateful for the giggles coming from the playroom, paint coming off his daughter at her bath at night. He'd been grateful that there had been no more escape attempts. In fact, Miss Carmichael and Genevieve appeared to be completely bonded over the Halloween project.

Now, his daughter—make that Chance—was dressed in a delightful costume, head to toe fluffy brown curls, a hood with ears, her brows thickened, her nose red and whiskers on her cheeks—and was running around him, barking excitedly.

He was wearing a plaid shirt and an oversize cowboy hat. The plaid shirt had been padded, as it would act as a jacket on a night that had turned quite cold. It made him look quite rotund.

But being fat was nothing on the final piece of the costume. It was a large cardboard box that had been transformed into a horse, the box its body, a cardboard cutout of a neck with a thick wool mane attached. At the end of the neck was a hand-painted horse's head, wild eyes and flaring nostrils, and a surprisingly good facsimile of reins and a bridle.

According to Miss Carmichael's instructions,

Drew stepped inside a hole in the top of the horse box and pulled it up. It was held in place around his waist with straps over his shoulders. False human legs, denim-clad and fat as sausages, ended in cowboy boots and stirrups. They had been attached to the outside of the box horse. Two false horse legs dragged along behind the box, and Drew's real legs were the horse's front legs.

It was really an ingenious contraption. And hilarious. A tubby guy in a too-large hat on a comical horse.

It was also completely without sex appeal. He had, without evidence, reached the incorrect conclusion that Genevieve was going to be Bobo Robbins, not him.

Not that he had thought about it, but if he had, he would have cast himself differently. A prince, maybe. Or a pirate.

A dashing and romantic hero who would have made Alexandra's mouth fall open and her eyes darken with lust.

Lust.

Maybe it wasn't too late to pick up a different costume somewhere on their way to the Halloween party. It wasn't that this one wasn't brilliant, it's just that Drew was not sure he was comfortable in a role so without dignity. Plus, this costume was going to attract attention. It would be so much easier to fade into the background as a Count Dracula or King Arthur.

On the other hand, this getup should protect him from anything even remotely lustful. He wouldn't be getting within three feet of another person with his box horse surrounding him like a suit of armor. Sneaking kisses would be out of the question.

He turned to look at Genevieve and Miss Carmichael. As he moved, the crazy legs attached to the horse flopped about madly in their stirrups. The girls were in absolute hysterics.

The new Drew—the one he had not been at the beginning of October—cast dignity aside in favor of that squealing laughter.

He rocked the box up and down as if the horse was bucking, and he held on to his hat as if he was in danger of being thrown off. He was rewarded with more laughter. He was aware Genevieve was looking at him with total delight and surprise.

Had he really become so dull? The dad who was absolutely no fun to be around? Maybe that's why Christmas in Lapland had been such a bust.

"Let's go, Chance," he said to Genevieve.

It was then he noticed that Miss Carmichael was dressed as the third member of the trio, the owl, Cowly.

He was aware, again, that the man he had been at the beginning of this month might not have noticed the intricacies of a costume she must have worked on for hours. He might not have noticed her eagerness, that she was just barely more than a child herself, still excited about Halloween.

"What are your plans for tonight?" he asked.

"Oh, I don't have any. Not really. I just made the costume for me because it was fun. It made Genevieve happy."

He thought of the giggles that had been coming from the playroom, a tired, contented little girl in the tub at night, the water turning blue and pink as the paint sluiced off her. It had, indeed.

That's what thawed hearts did. They made other people happy.

"Would you like to join us, Miss Carmichael?" he asked.

Her face lit up as if he had showered her with stardust and diamonds. That's what thawed hearts did. They felt the radiant warmth of moments when they gave other people joy. The feeling was addictive.

"It's Lila," she said shyly.

When they went outside, it was damp and foggy. Miserable.

"Perfect for Halloween," Lila told Genevieve, and his daughter beamed.

The car was waiting, and he removed his horse and it was placed carefully in the trunk. He got in beside the girls and gazed out at the New York skyline, just beginning to be smudged with the late-fall darkness.

What would having a heart this open mean

around Alexandra? It was all her fault that he was a different man than he had been a month ago, and to be honest, he did not know if he was resentful or grateful.

He did not know if accepting it was bravery or cowardice.

A two-block area had been closed to vehicular traffic, and the car dropped them at the corner.

"Can we go find Macy?" Genevieve asked, getting out of the car and hopping from foot to foot.

"Of course."

There were a lot of people here. He wanted to tell Miss Carmichael—Lila—to keep a close eye on Genevieve, but when he saw her hand close firmly around her small charge's, he knew it wasn't necessary.

They took off into the crowd and were soon lost in the fog.

He sighed, and his breath made a cloud in front of his mouth. He was glad that Genevieve's outfit looked warm and was thankful his own plaid shirt was padded against the cold. No, he didn't have to worry about Genevieve with Miss Carmichael. She had thought of everything.

The driver came around and opened the trunk and took out the horse. Drew carefully climbed in it, put the straps over his shoulders and gathered the reins.

"I must say, sir, best costume ever."

"I have to agree," he said.

"Never mind," the driver said hoarsely. "I've changed my mind."

Drew turned in the direction the driver was looking. His mouth fell open. The damp mist parted a bit, and he saw a vision in a hooded cloak was standing a few feet away and appeared to be watching them. She stood, frozen like a deer in headlights, as if at one move, she would turn and run.

Instead, she reached up and pulled the hood down. It took him a very long thirty seconds before he realized it was Alexandra.

And he was not sure he had any defenses against *that*.

Nor was he sure he wanted any.

He lifted a hand in greeting, and she came toward him. Alexandra was dressed as the sexy seductress from the hugely popular movie *Kiss of Death*. She was wearing a heavy black cape, fur lining the hood. As she came toward him, the cape swung open and revealed the blood-red dress underneath it. The dress clung to her like a film and had a plunging neckline. It was very short and revealed a stunning length of legs, clad in black fishnet stockings.

Her makeup, in keeping with the character, was exaggerated, but it made her eyes look as dark and as sensuous as a spell, and her lips look as tempting and juicy as a poison apple. Her hair had been braided into a single thick plait that fell over her right shoulder and made his fingers itch to unweave it.

People who believed in such things said that each good turn you did for another returned to you, a karmic gift.

He had not expected any kind of return when he'd invited Lila to come, but now he saw how that spontaneous invitation to the young nanny was returning something extraordinary to him.

He was free of all the normal Halloween responsibilities any dad might feel. Free to see where an evening with Shanna, the Sorceress, would lead.

The word *lust* appeared inside his head, bright as a sign made of neon tubing.

He was momentarily taken aback by it. He hadn't known her long, but certainly long enough to know she wasn't that kind of a woman. She had been consistently professional. He had seen how wholesome her family was. She had revealed to him she held a reservoir of pain at least as large as his own.

Except then they had shared that kiss.

That had changed everything.

And maybe Alexandra Harris was not the same woman she had been a month ago, either. Because Drew was pretty sure *that* woman would have never worn a dress—even if it was a costume—like the one she had on tonight.

If Drew hadn't spotted her, Alexandra might have, at the last moment, changed directions to run home to find a different costume. How had he managed to find a costume that was so light-hearted and *fun*? She had managed the exact opposite.

Though "managed" was a bit of an exaggeration. It had been a super-busy week. She'd had another meeting with Ivy, and she had also met with Hailey and seen samples of the first flowers for the wedding. Added to that, she'd put together the final details of a Halloween wedding, which had, thankfully, gone off without a hitch an hour ago.

With everything going on, however, she hadn't had time to plan a costume, and so she'd had to run into a store and grab the first costume she saw. Well, not exactly the *first* one, which had been Little Red Riding Hood. Instead, she'd looked right past that one and had gravitated to a rack of rather sexy items, no doubt spurred on by a kiss that she hadn't quite been able to put out of her mind for weeks, not matter how hard she worked, no matter how deeply she immersed herself in her world of creating perfect days and dreams come true for others.

She had almost lost her nerve when she'd first seen herself in this outfit, but then she'd talked herself into it. She didn't have time to change it. Now, she wished she'd slapped together something out of her own closet.

She had jeans and an old cowboy hat. Wouldn't that have looked cute with what he had on?

It would have been perfect. Safe, but perfect. On the other hand, something flashed through his eyes, white-hot, as he took in her costume. She was pretty sure a pair of jeans wouldn't have done that.

"That is the best costume ever," Alexandra told him.

"I disagree," he said, his voice gruff. "Yours is the best costume ever."

"Definitely yours, miss," the driver said, then ducked his head and slid into the car.

"You look like someone else completely," Drew said.

That's what she had told herself when she had looked in the mirror and seen the look was a little more over-the-top sexy than she had guessed it would be when she grabbed it off the rack.

Don't be chicken, Alexandra had told her reflection sternly. Wasn't that what wearing a costume was about? Giving yourself permission to be someone else?

Now, she wondered if a chicken might not have been better.

"Well," she said, "You don't exactly look like yourself, either. A perfect Bobo Robbins."

"You're familiar with my character," he said with a roll of his eyes.

"With the number of nieces and nephews I have? Of course. Who made it? It's brilliant."

She debated leaning in and giving him a kiss—just a little hello buss on the cheek—but she had chosen a crazy shade of red lipstick, and it would leave a mark on his cheek.

The thought of marking him—look, he's *mine*—had an odd appeal. Until she reminded herself she was related to half the people in this throng, and they would be making deliriously hopeful note of such things. They were going to make note of her outfit, too. She definitely should have thought this through more carefully.

And yet, after that kiss they had shared the last time they'd met, she wasn't feeling like she wanted to be careful. Was she feeling a little deliriously hopeful herself? For a repeat of last time?

Ridiculous.

"It turns out Miss Carmichael—Lila—helps make costumes for a theater group."

"Oh! I saw her and Genevieve race by me. Genevieve barely acknowledged me, though. She was rushing off to find Macy."

"Ah, Macy. I think there is a little case of hero worship unfolding there. I have her to thank, in a roundabout way, for the costume."

"You don't seem that enthused about your costume," she said. "And it's perfectly adorable."

"Do I look like a man who wants to be perfectly adorable?"

Her eyes drifted to his lips. "No," she admitted.

"I had pictured something a little more dashing. Or even sinister. Can you picture me as a villain?" He twirled an imaginary mustache and lowered his brow at her.

She could, indeed, picture him as a villain, the bad boy—the gunslinger, the pirate, the jewel thief—who created unwanted stirrings of longing in the pure, sweet hearts of every single good girl he ever met.

CHAPTER ELEVEN

"I DON'T CARE for villains," Alexandra told Drew primly, though in truth she had never considered whether she liked them or not. In the context of *him*, it was an absolute lie.

"Oh. Villains are out, then."

As if her opinion really mattered to him. Why would that create such an unexpected feeling of warmth in the region of her heart?

"Superman," he suggested. "A sheikh. A prince. How could that girl miss my potential so completely?"

As he said it, she could picture him in each of those roles *completely*. Unfortunately.

"She did what would make Genevieve happy," Alexandra said. "You have yourself a gem of a nanny there."

"Thanks to your intervention. So, no more complaining or conjecturing. I promise I will appreciate my costume completely." He pretended the horse was rearing up and swept off his hat to her.

Alexandra laughed, even as she made note of how dashing he was even in the silly costume. In fact, Alexandra thought it was probably a very good thing for both of them that his costume did not show off his full masculine charm.

They were going to put that kiss behind them. Become friends. Enjoy a really fun night with no strings and no complications. She couldn't even remember the last time she'd just given herself over to having lighthearted fun. She was pretty sure he couldn't, either.

Kisses, she reminded herself, were complications of the worst variety.

He pretended the horse was getting away from him, sidling sideways. She laughed more, and so did he, and it boded well for the evening.

They explored the block party. And it *was* fun. There was almost a giddiness to them, as if they were two children let loose at a country fair. Every house looked as if it had tried to outdo its neighbors with decorations. There were gravestones in front yards and skeletons hanging from roof peaks. There were inflatable werewolves and witches. The mistiness of the night was a perfect backdrop for all the spookiness.

They stopped at a bonfire, where there were vats of hot chocolate, hot dogs and freshly made candy and caramel apples. They admired costumes and were admired. Hordes of screaming, costumed children ran by them with loot bags filled with candy. Occasionally they would catch sight of Genevieve and Macy, still with Lila Carmichael.

They watched people bob for apples and each took a few blindfolded swipes at a huge pumpkin piñata. There were a couple of game booths raising money for charity, and despite how difficult it was for him to get his costume close to the counters, they played whack-a-witch, beanbag toss and spin-the-wheel.

Drew won Alexandra the homeliest stuffed toy she had ever seen, a plush warty toad. Winning it probably cost him the equivalent to a month's rent for her, but it wasn't the expense that made her aware she was going to treasure it forever. It was his tongue caught between his teeth in concentration—it was the fact that he wanted it so badly *for her*.

They ran into her sister, Heather, and her brother, Shaun, shepherding kids with pillowcases already filled with candy from house to house. Thankfully, introductions were brief. It looked as if Shaun desperately wanted to interrogate Drew, but there was too much chaos going on around them to encourage conversation.

Finally, just as the mist was turning to rain, they found themselves at the promised bouncy tent. It was filled with shrieking pint-size superheroes and ghosts, princesses and space creatures.

Shelley and Lila were outside it, and Macy and Genevieve were inside, holding hands, jumping facing each other.

"I'm going to take them home after this," Shelley told Drew and Alexandra. "They're just at that turning point—happiness to hysteria."

"*All* kids reach that turning point?" Drew asked.

"You poor man," Shelley said. "Of course they do. Usually once a day."

"Oh."

"It's not a failure on your part, believe me. Anyway, I'll grab them and put on a movie at home. I think they'll probably both be sleeping in minutes. Drew, you can come get her when you're ready to go." She looked from him to Alexandra. She looked at how Alexandra was dressed, and how she was clutching the toad. "Or you can leave her with me for the night."

Alexandra felt a Shanna the Sorceress desire to make her sister-in-law, who was being embarrassingly obvious about her hopes, disappear in a puff of smoke.

"I shouldn't impose on you. I should take her home—"

"No. Go enjoy."

He honestly looked like he did not know how. But after a moment, he said to Shelley, "Let me leave you my number, in case Genevieve wants to say good night."

After he had given out the phone number,

he turned to his nanny. "Miss Carmichael—Cowly—can I arrange a car for you?"

She waved her hand. "No. I'm great. I'll figure it out, but thanks, Mr. Parker."

"Well," he said, looking at Alexandra as they moved off. "This is unexpected. For the first time in four years, I find myself one hundred percent responsibility-free. Have you any ideas?"

It was starting to pour rain and it was putting an obvious damper on the party, not to mention his poor cardboard horse.

Alexandra was shocked to find herself leaning close to him. She whispered in his ear, "Well, yes, I do."

He raised an eyebrow at her.

"Would you like to come to my place?" Alexandra blushed. Did it sound as if she was propositioning him? Along with her rather outrageous outfit, who could blame him if he reached that conclusion? She could feel her cheeks turning red. Maybe she had on enough makeup that he wouldn't notice.

"I always watch a spooky movie on Halloween," she said hastily. Her tone was almost defensive.

He cocked his head at her. Okay, it was probably more than obvious that she—the artistic type and wedding planner—did not lean to this kind of movie.

"Just...just on Halloween," she stammered.

"And I live close to here. In case Genevieve needs you."

He was smiling slightly, as if he was enjoying her embarrassment.

"I just meant," she stumbled on, "it's starting to rain quite hard. It's going to ruin your costume."

"We can only hope!"

"But that's all Lila's hard work!"

"You are intent on showing me how to be a better man, aren't you?"

"Not really," she said. And then realized that could be interpreted incorrectly, too. Nice girl inviting bad boy back to her place. On Halloween. To watch scary movies. Which could lead to clutching at his arm and hiding her head against his chest.

Her eyes skittered to his chest. At least, for someone less disciplined than herself, of course.

"And yet I seem to be becoming a better man, despite myself." He said that almost to himself, then shook it off.

"I'll make popcorn," she said hastily, as if that somehow legitimized the whole invitation.

"Good idea," Drew said. "To get out of the rain. And to still be relatively close to Genevieve."

No, it wasn't. It was a bad idea. And like most bad ideas, it was nearly irresistible. He fell into step beside her, the horse's poor head drooping in the rain. The Halloween celebration was winding down quickly now that it was past the bedtimes of most of the little ones and the rain was starting in earnest. Teenagers were trying to set off fireworks, but the weather was not cooperating and their efforts fizzled weakly.

By the time they got to her place, a turn-of-the-century brownstone, they were both soaked. He carefully took off the somewhat wilted horse and set it in her narrow front hallway to dry. She took off the cloak.

The dress had been clingy before. Now it was damp and downright sinful. He suddenly didn't look like he thought this was such a good idea after all. She reached into her coat cupboard and pulled out a ratty old sweater, which she threw over the damp dress.

"Do you...do you want something?" she stammered.

His eyes went to her lips and then skittered away. They both wanted something. Oh, this had been such a bad idea. Why did she feel on fire?

"To put on?" she clarified hastily. "Your shirt is soaked. Not that I have any men's clothes—"

She was blushing again.

"Sure, if you've got something that might fit me, that would be great."

He stood in the hallway, dripping on the floor, while she went and looked. She found an extra-large T-shirt that she sometimes used as summer pajamas.

The hallway seemed very cramped as she

handed him the shirt. Was that steam rising off him? Or was it rising off her?

"What can I get you?" she asked, her tone strangled, backing out of the entrance cubicle as he began to undo the buttons of his soggy shirt. "Coffee? Wine? Soda? A Rockingbird?"

He laughed. He had laughed a lot tonight, and she loved the sound of it. She suspected his laugh—and the way he looked when he laughed—had a lot to do with that feeling of fire burning inside her. With all that heat, no wonder her tiny front entryway was getting steamy.

"I've sworn off Rockingbirds. For life. Whatever you think goes with popcorn will be great."

What a wise choice, she thought, given how much she loved the sound of his laughter. No alcohol. No lowering of inhibitions.

"Soda it is." She left the front vestibule quickly. She ordered herself not to look back. And yet, she did. She caught a glimpse of the absolute male perfection of his naked back as he turned away from her and stripped off that wet shirt.

He was not perfectly adorable anymore. Just perfect.

His shoulders were wide, and his back was broad and sculpted. She loved the composition of it, the slight jut of back ribs, how his back narrowed where it disappeared into his pants. His chilled skin was marbled with goose bumps.

The artist in her appreciated him and wanted

to draw him, just like that. Standing there, shirtless, light spilling over his shoulders, unaware his masculine beauty was being watched.

No, it was more than wanting to draw him. She wanted to touch him. To explore his skin with her fingertips, to *know* the surface of him completely. Her awareness was so sharp it felt like hunger, and it rippled through her.

As if he could feel her energy vibrating through the air, he glanced over his shoulder and caught her staring at him.

She waited to turn into a pillar of salt, the way that women did when they were caught looking at things they weren't supposed to look back at.

She felt like a lot of things, but a pillar of salt was not one of them! She scurried into the bathroom and washed most of the Shanna the Sorceress makeup off her face. Then she went to her tiny kitchen and busied herself making popcorn. Her hands were trembling as she poured kernels into hot oil, and it wasn't all because she had gotten too cold on the walk home.

"Nice place," he called to her.

She knew it was a nice place. Why did it matter so much what he thought of it? And yet, it did matter what he thought of it, and she liked that when she came back in with the tray of popcorn and drinks, instead of sitting down, he wandered around looking at the art on her walls.

"You can tell an artist lives here."

"I'm a wedding planner, not an artist."

"Humph," he said. Why did it feel as if he was seeing who she really was?

"I like the way everything is put together. There's a sense of *you* in this space. Of home. I don't think I've ever quite achieved that."

He looked as if he thought he'd revealed too much about himself, and maybe he had, because it didn't really matter how much success a person had achieved—it didn't matter if they lived in New York's answer to a royal palace—if they didn't have a place that felt like home.

"Did you do these?" Drew paused in front of a series of paintings that she'd done at the family summer place when she was young.

"Yes."

The T-shirt was too small for him. It pulled tight over his shoulders, his biceps, the depth of his chest. Her awareness of him felt as if it would shatter her.

"They're really good," he said, sinking down on one end of the sofa. "I like the one of the dog on the dock, snoozing."

"Thank you." Her voice was normal, as if she wasn't vibrating with tension. She should have taken the chair across from him. She didn't. It was practical. She wouldn't be able to see the movie from the chair.

She set down the tray and took the other end of the sofa. "We had a cottage when I was growing up. We'd take out the canoe, and the dog would wait for us to get back."

The couch was extra tiny, because of the space. A love seat, really. Who named these things? "Let's put on the movie!" she said.

They perused a number of titles and picked one that sounded the worst: *Hatchets for Halloween*.

Alexandra promised herself she would not be scared. She would just see the silliness of it. She vowed off any bicep clutching or head burrowing.

At first, it was funny. They laughed at the poor acting and the terrible premise. They pointed out the outrageous choices and improbable setups.

But then, despite all the flaws, it was scary and she yelped with fright in spite of herself. Somehow, the popcorn bowl was moved, and Drew was right beside her, his arm over her shoulder. Somehow, she was burrowing under his arm and hiding her eyes.

"You know," he said, an hour later, when the movie had deteriorated into a bloodbath of not-very-good special effects, "I'm not married to it, if you want to shut it off. I'm afraid you're going to have bad dreams."

She shut off the movie very quickly. The silence after all the shrieking on-screen was a relief. She waited for him to move his arm off her shoulder, but he didn't.

It felt so good to be cuddled under his arm that

she didn't move, either. She savored the sense of being cared about, being protected in some delightful way.

He leaned his head on the back of her sofa and closed his eyes. "Thank you for tonight. I feel like it was my first real Halloween."

She let her eyes wander the column of his throat, rest on the hump of his Adam's apple, move on to the tantalizing texture of whiskers thickening on his face. Very villain-like, those whiskers. Though not anything like the villain in the movie, thank goodness.

"Your first true Halloween as a daddy?" she asked, trying to clarify what he had just said. "It was probably the first year of real trick or treating for Genevieve, wasn't it?"

CHAPTER TWELVE

LET HER BELIEVE THAT, Drew ordered himself. But he'd noticed, around Alexandra, his customary self-discipline fled him. "I meant for me."

There it was, Drew thought. Even though Alexandra had covered up the sorceress dress, he felt as if he was under a spell. When he'd pulled on that shirt in her front hallway and turned and seen her looking at him, it had felt as if the bottom was falling out of his world.

The whole evening had been so laughter-filled, carefree. There had been a feeling in the air, a community celebrating. Families being together. Loving being together.

Her house intensified that feeling. *Home*. That series of paintings called to something in him. The ramshackle cottage with a hammock on the porch. A clothesline, strung tree to tree, with colorful, worn towels hanging on it. An old, loyal dog who waited for the family.

Of course Alexandra had grown up like this. She had grown up in a neighborhood that held

Halloween parties. And knew what to do to make
Christmas magic. They probably had Easter egg
hunts, too.

An awareness crystallized in Drew. All his life,
he had longed for *this*. It felt like the weakness,
left unguarded, would destroy him. It seemed to
him it was a defect, that he could bring nothing to
her world. She needed to know *all* of him if they
were going to follow that look that had passed
between them when he had stripped off his wet
shirt in her hallway.

If they were going to follow what he felt with
her trembling, and letting out little yelps of fear,
and hiding under his arm from that dreadful
movie.

She made him feel like a man in a way he had
not for a long, long time.

"What do you mean?" she asked uncertainly.
"Didn't you have Halloween at the orphanage?"

"I said I was an orphan," he told her. "I never
said I grew up in an orphanage."

"Oh. No, you didn't. For some reason, I just
assumed."

"I dreamed of an orphanage when I was a kid.
I thought it would be full of other children. Rambunctious activity. Hijinks. Friends. Coconspira-
tors in escape attempts. Maybe we'd even all be
conscripted into a band of thieves by a Fagin-like
character."

Did he sound self-pitying? He did not want

to say these things. Why was he saying these things? Her nearness was drawing a long-ago whimsy from him. Her space—so cozy, though maybe a touch too warm—was drawing secrets from him.

You had to be careful around a woman like her. He knew that. And yet he could not summon caution.

"My parents died in a car accident when I was seven. What I remember the most was how they were with each other. Always laughing. Touching. Exchanging looks. It was the kind of love that excluded everything—and everybody—else.

"My dad had a sister who took me. My aunt Sarah. She was older than him. A college professor in a small town. She didn't believe in *nonsense*. Which included Christmas, Halloween and Easter."

He smiled and could feel the faint bitterness in it as he imitated her voice. "'Bunnies and bearded men. What are we teaching children?' She had her own ideas about what children should learn. I didn't really have friends my own age. I had her friends. I was included in adult discussions. It had its good points, but—"

"But it's horrible being treated like an adult when you're a kid," she said firmly.

"Emily's childhood was even worse than mine. She *was* raised in an orphanage. In Eastern Europe. Together, we thought we'd find our way. We wanted to give Genevieve the childhood neither of us ever had. We thought we could fix it somehow for the next generation."

"You can," she whispered.

He opened his eyes. She had crept very close to him. He could feel her warmth. He felt like a sailor who had been lost at sea and finally spotted a lighthouse.

"I can't," he said. "I realize that now. I realized it tonight. I don't know the first thing about it. I don't even know how to have fun. There's something else my aunt believed."

Don't say it. He begged himself not to say it.

"She believed love caused the worst kind of pain. I think she adored my father. I think she felt excluded from that love he had for my mom. As if she had lost him. And, in some way, I think she felt their love was responsible for their deaths. My dad, her younger brother, was the only light in her small, dark little world.

"But, still, when I met Emily, I thought my aunt was wrong. So wrong. She would look at us together, and instead of being happy for us, she'd give a warning—*people can love too much.* She died, of old age and crankiness, before Emily did. Before," he said softly, "she ever found out how right she was."

"She wasn't right," Alexandra said.

He opened his eyes, expecting to feel ashamed

of all he had just said, like someone who blurts out their life story to a stranger on a bus.

But when he looked at her, it didn't feel as though she was a stranger. It felt as if he knew her. It felt as if some burden that he had carried alone was suddenly lighter. Was that fair to Alexandra? To lighten his burden at her expense?

But there was something fierce in her as she gazed steadily back at him. Something compelling. Something a man could lean toward, grab, hang on to.

At some point, he wasn't sure when, she had washed all that makeup off. Incredibly, she was more a sorceress without it.

"She wasn't right about anything," Alexandra said, not the same woman who had been hiding under his arm a little while ago. She was strong now, like a warrior, sure of herself. "Not about loving too much. Not about everything fun being nonsense."

Her fierceness was like a warm light flickering on a cold night. He still had his arm around her shoulder. He was suddenly so aware of how she fit against him, how *right* it felt where their bodies were pressed together, side by side.

He relished the warmth of her like a man who had lost his way on a bitter night, when the cold was killing, and who had been so close to giving up hope.

When her lips touched his, there was nothing

fun about it. Nothing at all. He felt everything that had been frozen in him shatter. The layers of protection around him had felt so strong, so impenetrable. Now he saw that what he had considered to be a fortress had really only been the thinnest layer of ice. It fell away from him in fragile, broken shards.

His hands found the thick plait in her hair, and he did what he had wanted, at some primal level, to do all night. He removed the band from the end of it and then inserted his fingers deep into the plaits and tugged softly as he ran his hands down the length of her hair. The plait dissolved. Her hair was wavy from it, and it fell, freed, in a magnificent wave to the luscious swell of her breast.

He accepted the invitation of her lips with all the desperation, all the urgency of a man saved from a cold and lonely death.

In exploring the softness of her lips, the moist, warm cavern of her mouth, a new awareness exploded within him.

Drew didn't just want to live. He didn't just want to go through the motions, of breathing in and out, of getting up each day, of trying to be a great dad, of trying to figure out what was best for his little girl.

He wanted to be alive.

He tangled with her: his hands in her hair, his tongue with her tongue, his body up against hers.

He reveled in how, even as they fit so perfectly together, there were magnificent contrasts between them. Soft. Hard. Smooth. Jagged. Gentle. Rough.

For one brief moment in time, he was just a man. Primitive. Wanting what she offered. No, more. Needing.

His world became only sensation. Only him. And only her. The rest of the world at bay, outside this white-hot circle they had created.

She took his hand and gently guided it to the end of that cascading wave of hair, to her breast beneath it. The white-hot heat intensified. An inferno that could consume them both.

He could feel the beat of her heart and the whisper of her breath. He looked into the soft suede brown of her eyes and saw the tender, fierce invitation there.

But then, something penetrated it all. A whisper. A reminder he did not have the luxury—not anymore—of living solely for himself.

He did not have the luxury of wildly pursuing pleasure.

There was a responsibility that outweighed all other considerations. What was best for his little girl?

What did being a daddy require of him? Decency. Honor.

He moved back from Alexandra. He broke the contact between them. It felt like just about the hardest thing he had ever done, especially when she looked at him, her expression dazed, confused, hurt.

This raw passion, this need, felt so right, but it was wrong. It was wrong for her, this woman who had grown up with cottages and Christmas trees, and it was wrong for Genevieve.

This was not what he wanted to teach his daughter about life.

This was not what he wanted her to accept from a man one day. Passion without commitment.

He pulled completely away from Alexandra. He could see he had wounded her. He could see she read it as rejection.

"We can't," he said. "Not like this. Alexandra, we barely know each other."

That felt, weirdly, like a lie. He felt as if he knew Alexandra to the core. As if he knew her heart and her soul. He didn't feel as if he had met her weeks ago, but a lifetime ago. Or maybe even several lifetimes ago, if a person believed in that sort of thing.

She ran a hand through the gorgeous mess of her hair. Her lips were swollen. Her eyes were wide, and if he wasn't mistaken, a tiny diamond of a tear was forming in the corner of one of them.

She looked utterly crushed. This was the danger of not closing doors completely. It could crush her more to follow these threads of desire. It could crush them both.

"We have to slow it down," he said. His voice was ragged with thwarted desire.

But he could not close the door, not completely. He wanted what he had felt when he kissed her. He wanted to feel alive. She did, too. Both of them had been damped down by the burdens they carried for way too long.

Of course there was risk. He knew there was risk. She knew there was risk. You could not get through life without risk.

He threw her the lifeline, the very same way she had thrown it to him.

"You're right, of course," she said, looking deeply embarrassed. "I don't know what I was thinking. As you said, we barely know each other."

"But we can change that," he said softly. It felt like the biggest chance he had ever taken, the most dangerous risk. And the most glorious. "Let's get to know each other."

Her eyes flew to his face, searching.

"Yes, of course," she said, and she moved away from him, shoved her hair out of her face, made a move like she was going to get up.

He wanted to do the honorable thing. But he couldn't quite let go of her, either. He caught her hand and pulled her back to him. He guided her head back onto his chest.

His hand went to the back of her head, as if he could pull her in even closer to his heart. He felt her hair, stroked it, and a finely held tension dissolved slowly in her as her muscles relaxed against him. Her breath grew deep and formed a pool of warmth on his chest.

He knew if he went to sleep like this, he was going to wake up with a sore neck in the morning.

Somehow, it didn't matter. He could not bring himself to move out from under the sweet weight of her.

His eyes closed and he slept the deep, untroubled sleep of a man who knew he might be flawed, and he might make mistakes as a dad every single day, but in the end he had the most important quality of all. He could be trusted to do the right thing.

Alexandra startled awake to a vibration right in her ear. She had been fast asleep on Drew's chest and realized it must be a phone going off in his shirt pocket. And if she was not mistaken, that was a little pool of drool next to said shirt pocket.

As if she didn't have enough to be embarrassed about! She'd lost control last night. Completely. Had she actually taken his hand and… She went crimson just thinking about it.

He's the one who had stopped it. With some variation of *We should just be friends*. Really, it was too embarrassing for words. She should just creep off and lock herself in the bathroom until he was gone.

On the other hand, he was still here. Did that mean something?

He was stirring, and it was too late to make her escape, so she sat up, and with all the dignity she could manage she ran her hand through her hair and acted as if everything was completely fine. It would have been easier if the motion didn't make her think of his hands in it, unweaving the braid.

Out of the corner of her eye, she watched him come to life, disoriented, slapping at his shirt as if the buzzing was coming from a bothersome bee.

His hair, always so tidy, was sticking straight up. His whiskers had darkened around his face.

She wanted to touch both. Which wasn't, apparently, within the parameters of *We have to slow down* and *Let's get to know each other*, which, in the watery light of a new day, she read to mean Drew Parker wanted a platonic relationship, even if he had stayed the night.

With her slobbering away on his chest.

He'd found the phone and scowled at it. "I don't know this number. Damnably early for telemarketers."

Alexandra glanced at his phone. "It's Shelley."

He answered quickly.

"Daddy?" Alexandra could hear Genevieve's voice, excited and happy, no worse the wear for her night away from her dad.

"Good morning, sweetheart."

Did he have to say it like that? As if a light

had come on in his world? Alexandra was trying to maintain some of her composure, keep her distance from him. It was much harder to do when witnessing that tenderness for his daughter in his tone.

He laughed. "No, it's not Christmas, it's the day after Halloween."

This was followed by a stream of chatter that Alexandra couldn't make out. Drew shot her a look and put the phone against his chest. "It seems I'm getting an early start on Christmas fails this year."

He put the phone back up to his ear. "Okay, okay," he finally said, exasperated. "It's Christmas. What do you mean, go look?"

He lifted a shoulder at Alexandra. "She says we have to go look out the window. That it's Christmas."

She loved that he was indulging Genevieve. She loved the little girl's insistent belief. She loved that they both got up and went to the window, where the shades were still drawn tight.

"Are you ready?" Alexandra said, fingers on the cord of the blind. Such was the power of Genevieve's belief that Alexandra half expected to see a sleigh and reindeer outside her window.

As she rolled up the shade, her mouth fell open. At some point, last night's rain had turned to snow. The world had turned into a magical place, sparkling, clean, brand-new. She felt Drew looking at her.

She was aware her hair was wavy from the braid and terribly tangled. Her sweater was lumpy. There was a slobber spot on his shirt, and no doubt the pattern of that shirt was imprinted on her cheek. So the look on his face—the look of wonder—had to be because of the snow.

Not because he had woken up beside a woman he wanted to slow things down with.

"It's snowman weather," Alexandra said to keep herself from blurting that he was the most handsome man she had ever woken up beside. Of course, that would be an exclusive club of two, one of those being her ex-husband.

Drew was still holding the phone, and Genevieve heard her. She didn't ask why her daddy was with Alexandra, or even seem surprised by it. Her sigh came over the phone.

"That's *exactly* what I thought," his daughter said dreamily. "Can we build a snowman today?"

"Of course," he said. "I'll be over to get you soon." He disconnected, and his gaze settled on Alexandra. "You'll come, won't you? You probably know a lot more about snowmen than I do."

"It's hardly rocket science," she said, a touch grouchily. She'd only been invited to join them because she might be an expert on something as nonthreatening as building a snowman. It was the type of activity you invited the person you'd relegated as your platonic friend to do with you.

She suddenly felt ashamed of herself as a light bulb went on inside her. The reason for his rejection was obvious to her—Drew Parker still loved his wife.

CHAPTER THIRTEEN

DREW PARKER STILL loved his wife, and he wasn't ready to move on. Alexandra told herself that wasn't something to take personally. If anything, his ability to love so deeply was admirable.

When had she become *this* person, who could look at a single dad, in hopelessly over his head— he already thought he was failing at Christmas— and his adorable little daughter, and say, *If there's nothing in it for me, if you can't love me the way I can love you, forget it?*

Love?

Where had that thought come from? She didn't love him. He was absolutely right. They hadn't known each other long enough for that.

So, she lusted after him.

There it was. The truth—as ugly as a bad Christmas sweater—that he had managed, ever so sensibly, to head off at the pass last night.

If anyone should know what a bad road lust was to follow, it should be her. She needed to be a better person than she had ever been before.

She vowed to be. She sucked in her breath. She drew back her shoulders.

She looked at the green of his eyes, and the muss of his hair, and the stubble on his chin. She remembered his breath stirring her hair and his lips laying claim to her.

"I've got a very busy day," she said. What had happened to her vow to be a better person? Life had a way of testing vows.

And then it tested them yet further.

He lifted a shoulder, letting her know whatever worked for her was okay. "Do you mind if I use your shower?"

"No, of course not."

But then when she went into the shower, still steamy from him, it was as if wisps of him were in there with her. His scent, his masculinity—his nudity in this very space just moments ago—floating around her, teasing her, taunting her, tormenting her.

There was no sense trying to look gorgeous for a man who just wanted a platonic relationship, but still, she put on makeup. She blow-dried and curled her hair. She was way too careful in her selection of a creamy angora sweater, flattering narrow-legged pants.

It was good that he'd set a limit, Alexandra thought as she looked at herself in the mirror, her dark hair spilling over her shoulder in sweet contrast to the lightness of the sweater. She recognized that now. But she wouldn't be human if she didn't want Drew Parker to regret it.

A few minutes later, Alexandra took a deep breath as she went up Shaun and Shelley's front step. Drew's hair was still wet from the shower, and he was wearing the same padded plaid jacket he'd been wearing last night.

Her brother and sister-in-law were going to draw inevitable conclusions.

She knocked at the door and went in without waiting for someone to answer it, as was their custom at each other's houses.

Genevieve, in a pair of borrowed pajamas, rocketed across the room, and Drew scooped her up.

"I had the best time *ever*," she squealed.

Alexandra did not miss the slightly pained look on Drew's face at that announcement. He was a man who had, quite literally, gone to the ends of the earth to give his daughter the best time ever. And somehow, she'd had it without him.

Shaun padded out of the kitchen, munching on a piece of toast. He was eyeing Drew with way too avid interest.

"It's not what you think," Alexandra whispered at him in an undertone.

He raised an eyebrow at her and made absolutely no attempt to follow her lead and keep a confidential tone of voice.

"I'll always be your big brother, but honestly, Alex, you're thirty-one years old."

She glanced at Drew and blushed. Good grief. Her brother *wanted* her to have an affair. He'd probably be as disappointed as she was if he knew about the very platonic nature of her evening.

But then she realized, that's not what Shaun wanted. Not at all.

He wanted her happiness.

He wanted it in the same way, she realized, she wanted it for Genevieve and Drew. And for the first time in a long time, for herself, too.

Could her happiness be intertwined with theirs? Even if she had the hots for Drew and he did not seem to return the sentiment? What if, for once in her life, she just took a chance?

She did something she hadn't done, not even once, since she had started her business. She fished her cell phone out of her bag and called the office.

"I won't be in today," she said. She waited for the protests, the questions, the *need*, and felt irritated when it didn't come.

"Did you just take the day off work?" Drew asked, smiling. In that smile, already it felt as if her gamble with happiness was paying off.

"Yes," she said.

"To build a snowman?"

"Yes. This kind of snow has a way of disap-

pearing fast." There. That should show him. It
was about the *snow*.

"Then why are you glaring at your phone like
that?" Drew asked.

"Quite insultingly, no one seems to think the
world of weddings is going to fall apart if I take
the day off."

"I guess Miss Carmichael can have the day off,
too," Drew said, and then he laughed. "And me."

Happiness gathered in the air and fell toward
them, like fairy dust.

An hour later, after going back to her house to
retrieve snow clothes, Alexandra stood inside
the door of Drew's private quarters, trying not
to gawk like a peasant granted entrance to the
palace.

He had been right last night when he had con-
fided in her that he had never quite achieved the
ambience of home in his space.

It was beautiful, no question, with its gorgeous
interiors: soaring ceilings and huge arched windows that looked toward the park. The decor
echoed what she had seen in the public spaces
of Parker and Parker. It was opulent, with knotted
silk rugs, expensive paintings and exquisite furniture. But, even with the odd toy on the floor, it
seemed more like a movie set—where the script
read, *extremely wealthy person's house*—than a

real home, where people laughed and played and spilled juice on the couch.

"Come help me with my snowsuit," Genevieve insisted, tugging on her hand.

"Yes," Drew said, "you go help her. I'll see what I can dig up for snowman accessories."

Genevieve's room was truly lovely: a princess room with a canopied bed and hand-painted bunnies on the walls.

Alexandra remembered Drew saying his aunt had disapproved of *nonsense* in general, and bunnies in particular, and so she loved it that he had given his little girl a room filled with whimsy.

The snowsuit was tucked into a large closet, and Alexandra helped stuff Genevieve into it. She had helped with snowsuits dozens of times with her nieces and nephews, but she was not sure she had ever quite felt like this before.

She had a tenderness for the motherless little girl that made her heart feel as if it was swelling unreasonably.

They met Drew in the hallway. He had found mittens and hats and scarves, both for the snowman and him and Genevieve.

He looked utterly dashing, with a woolen hat pulled on and a scarf wrapped around his throat, like the star of a Christmas movie, or the model for the front cover of a romance novel.

Alexandra didn't think she looked quite as appealing in her padded jacket and bulky snow pants she'd pulled over the pants she had selected so carefully this morning. She might as well not have bothered finding an attractive outfit. Unlike Drew—poster boy for winter fun—she looked ungainly.

"I look like the fat little baker on bread bags," she said.

Genevieve and Drew both eyed her appraisingly. "More like the tire man," Genevieve decided, and Drew's laughter was almost worth sacrificing a sexy look for.

"You have the best front yard in all of New York," Alexandra told Drew once they were in the snow-covered park. Parker and Parker soared behind them, regal, as picturesque as a winter-bound castle in a fairy tale.

"I want a big snowman, Daddy."

"Here," he said, "let me show you how to start it. You make a little ball like this, and then you set it on the ground and roll it."

Just as Alexandra had suspected this morning, the snow was perfect for building snowmen, sticky and wet. Genevieve was soon totally engrossed in the pure magic of creating the snowball. It quickly gained size, leaving a trail of bare ground behind it.

Alexandra and Drew both started their own, but soon the balls were too heavy for one person to move and they had to be on the same team. They joined Genevieve. She had given up and was resting her back against her snowball, eating snow off her mitten.

With Genevieve between Alexandra and Drew, at first they were able to roll it with their hands, but it got even larger and they put their shoulders to it. They grunted. Laughed. Slipped. Fell. And then pushed some more.

Finally, they were all satisfied with the first ball of the snowman. They joined together on the ball Alexandra had started and pushed it.

When it finally rested against the base of the snowman, Alexandra realized the second ball was nearly as big as the first.

The three of them stood there gazing at it.

"I think it might be a little too ambitious," Alexandra offered.

"What does that mean?" Genevieve asked.

"It's too heavy to lift up."

"My daddy's really strong," Genevieve told Alexandra seriously. "He's probably the strongest man in the world. He can do it."

"Yeah," Drew said, throwing Alexandra a look. He crouched in front of the ball. He put his arms on either side of it, he deepened his squat and then he straightened his legs.

Some of the snow shaved away, but the ball did not move.

Alexandra giggled. She put on her Olympic announcer voice and said solemnly, "And it looks like Parker's first attempt at this weight has failed."

Drew sent her a dark look and squatted again.

In her announcer voice, Alexandra said, "Ignoring the possibility of personal injury, Parker is going to make a second attempt at the lift. Quiet from the audience, please. Intense concentration will be required."

He shot her another dirty look and got himself ready. With a shout worthy of that fictional Olympic weight lifter, he pulled up with all his strength. The ball actually wobbled and lifted a full inch off the ground, but then he lost his grip on it, and staggered backward, falling on his backside. The snowball broke in two. One half crumbled completely.

"Daddy, you broke it," Genevieve said accusingly.

"It looks like a clear disqualification for Parker," Alexandra announced solemnly.

He glared at both of them as he scrambled to his feet and brushed off his rather delectable derriere. For a man who wanted to go slow, he shouldn't be drawing that kind of attention to himself. He twirled what she assumed was an imaginary mustache and gave a villainous and menacing chortle.

Drew leaned back over and scooped up some of the crumbled snow. His eyes fixed on Alexandra, he rotated the snow in his gloved hands, taking his time, shaping it.

Alexandra read his intent. "It's not my fault you were disqualified."

She could clearly see they were past the point of reasoning, so she took off running. The snowball splatted in the middle of her back. Laughing, she turned back to him and made her own menacing face. She scooped up a handful of snow and compacted it into a ball that was satisfyingly hard and should fly like a missile. She ran toward him and let it loose, right at his face. He ducked, and it missed.

She ducked behind Genevieve, using her as a shield but keeping the little girl supplied with snowballs.

Chortling madly, Genevieve threw them at Drew.

"Get him, Gen!" Alexandra called, crouched behind her, peeking out from behind the snowsuit.

How sweet was it that, over and over again, he would come close enough to let Genevieve's snowballs hit him. He put on such a great show of being grievously wounded that soon both Genevieve and Alexandra were helpless with laughter.

He took advantage of their distraction, filling both his arms with snow and coming and dumping the whole load over their heads. They got up and went after him. The snowballs, the yelled threats and the shouts of laughter were flying through the air. They ran through the heavy snow until they were breathless, until Alexandra could run no more.

"I surrender," she gasped, going down on her knees. She held out a snowball in her hands. "Take my sword."

Genevieve swooped in and grabbed it and threw it at her dad. And then, giggling, she came and lay beside her. Drew came and lay on the other side of Genevieve.

"I don't know which I like best," Genevieve said with a sigh. "Halloween or Christmas."

Their breath formed clouds above them, and happiness shimmered in the air around them. But they were soaked, and lying in the snow wasn't helping. Genevieve shivered.

"Come on," Drew said. "Let's finish the snowman and go for hot chocolate." He got to his feet.

Alexandra closed her eyes before he did the brushing part. When she opened them, he was standing above her. He offered his hand. And she took it.

He pulled her to her feet with just a little more force than was strictly necessary, and she found herself thrust against the full length of him.

She looked up at him. His gaze, despite the playfulness of what they had just been through, was smoldering. He let her go.

"We can't finish him," Genevieve said, inspecting the snowman. "We made him too big."

"Ha!" Drew said, "Your dad may not have brawn, but he has brains."

"What's brawn?" Genevieve asked.

Alexandra thought of the ease with which he had just pulled her to him. She thought of how his naked chest had looked in her front hallway last night. That was brawn, not that she felt inclined to explain it to the child.

Drew went and inspected the snowman. He salvaged the broken ball, pasting it back together with more snow. And then, engineer that he was, he started building a ramp to roll the ball up. Soon, Alexandra and Genevieve had joined him in the engineering project.

But as it turned out, it was completely unnecessary. Three teenage boys came along and, without being asked, picked up the second ball and plopped it easily on top of the first one.

"Utterly humiliating," Drew told her with a self-deprecating grin, watching the boys saunter away. "This is really no way to impress a lady."

He'd had his chance to impress her last night and had taken a miss. But she found she couldn't sacrifice the utter magic of this moment by dwelling on that one. Besides, was there really anything more impressive than watching a man delight his daughter?

CHAPTER FOURTEEN

GENEVIEVE WASN'T TALL enough to help put the head on the snowman, but Drew and Alexandra managed to get it placed and snow-glued it firmly to the second ball. And then Drew put Genevieve on his shoulders and handed her the bag he had brought. She put on the finishing touches: a red licorice cord mouth, a carrot nose, two Oreo cookies for eyes and more for buttons over the round snowman belly.

Drew took off his own hat and scarf and put them on the snowman.

"Those are too good for a snowman," Alexandra protested.

He shrugged. "If they're still here after the snowman melts, I'll come retrieve them. If not, I hope somebody who needs them gets them."

With great foresight, he had brought extra cookies. They stood back munching and admiring the snowman, and then Alexandra took out her cell phone and took pictures of Drew and Genevieve posing proudly with their creation.

And then, laughing, they took some selfies before Genevieve insisted on taking one of Drew and Alexandra.

Alexandra stood on one side, turned sideways, lifted one foot and kissed the snowman's cheek.

"Daddy, you do that, too."

And so they both kissed the snowman's cheek. And then, unexpectedly, with a whoop of pure joy, Drew came and picked Alexandra up and twirled her around, and then kissed her cheek when he set her back down.

It was all very platonic. Not at all worthy of the shiver of awareness that went through her like a bolt of fire.

"Time for hot chocolate?" he asked.

"Yes!" Genevieve said.

"I think I'm too wet," Alexandra said. She was soaked through in the bulky snow pants and jacket, right to her skin, and had already started to shiver.

But was that from being wet, or was it from the light shimmering inside her from the simple joy of being here, together, with Drew and Genevieve, like a small family?

It made her achingly aware that they wanted different things. It was time for her to break away from this before she wanted too much.

"We can go to my place," he said. "I have some dry things you can throw on."

So, there she would be again. Intimate. Sharing

his space. His clothes. Watching his lips. Wanting to touch his whiskers. She had to go home. Maybe she'd go home, have a nice hot bath and then drop into the office, after all. She had two weddings coming up this weekend. She also wanted to touch base with Hailey.

"Please, come," Genevieve said.

The plea in her voice was hard to resist. Plus, it was a reminder, that no, they didn't want all different things. They wanted some of the same things. His little girl's happiness, for one.

And so she was just going to have to suck it up to achieve that.

But as they trudged through the wet snow back to his place, Genevieve between them holding their hands and swinging, she was aware she didn't exactly feel the dull weight of a person doing their best to suck it up.

No, she felt the guilty exhilaration of someone who knew it was wrong but still couldn't stop playing with fire.

Genevieve got tired partway back to his place and held out her arms. Drew picked her up easily, and she fell asleep almost instantly.

"I think it's just too much," he told Alexandra. "Christmas falling so closely to Halloween. There's a reason these events have a break between them."

They both laughed.

"I'm going to go take her wet clothes off and

put her in something dry. I have a feeling—even though she's way too old for naps—she may be out for the count. Do you still want to come in?"

There was no excuse to say yes. The little girl, whose happiness was in question, was fast asleep. There were weddings to look after, meetings to hold, clients to reassure and coddle.

Alexandra realized she was already in way over her head when she found she could not say no.

He carried Genevieve up the stairs and indicated with a tilt of his chin that Alexandra should follow him.

"You'll find dry clothes in there," he said. "Closet, top drawer, far cabinet."

She went through the door and realized it was his bedroom. It was very grand and very tidy. The bed was huge, masculine, the bedding, in subtle shades of gray, sumptuous.

Trying not to be too much a voyeur, she went through to his closet. It was about the same size as her entire living room. It was a dressing room, really, with built-in cabinets, suits hanging neatly, color-coordinated shirts on top rungs, knife-pressed pants on the bottom ones. There was a huge island in the middle of the room, a stainless-steel washer and dryer tucked under it. She slid open one of the drawers to see rows of silk ties.

It was the space, she realized, of a man with no secrets. No one who had anything to hide would ever send someone into their bedroom. Or their closet. For some reason the fact he was so open endeared him to her.

As if she needed to like him any more.

She went to the far cabinet and slid open the drawer. It felt strangely intimate to shed her wet clothes. She was wet right through to her underwear, and so she took that off, too, and tossed it in the dryer. She put on one of his T-shirts and a pair of flannel pajama bottoms over naked skin. Both items were way too large, but it also felt good to be dry. And to have her skin surrounded by *him*, his scent clinging, ever so subtly, to the clothing.

She padded down the hall and found him just tucking his deeply sleeping daughter into her bed. He picked up her stuffy—a bunny—and popped it in beside her.

"I see you found what you needed," he said.

She was aware she did not look sexy. At all. And yet the look in his eyes made her feel sexy, which was irritating and confusing, because it was not the look of a man who just wanted to be friends.

"How about if you go rummage around my kitchen while I find something dry?" He nodded in the direction Alexandra should go.

His kitchen, like the rest of his house, was like something out of a photo shoot. But unlike the open concept that was so popular these days, it was tucked in behind the living room, a spacious bright room that looked as if it was rarely used.

Still, it was well stocked, and Alexandra found all the things to make hot chocolate. He came in just in time to pick up the tray and carry it out to the living room.

She took a seat on the couch. He went over to the fireplace and began to ball up paper and add kindling.

It was a good thing he'd made it clear this wasn't going anywhere, because otherwise a woman could make the mistake of thinking it was all very romantic.

Then Alexandra noticed the photo in the frame on the rough-hewn mantel. It was of a very beautiful woman, masses of dark curls falling around an exquisite face. She was very like Genevieve, and Alexandra knew instantly who it was.

Had she allowed herself to think—because he had stayed the night, because he didn't seem to want the day to end any more than she did—that maybe this was going somewhere after all?

The fire crackled to life.

Drew turned and looked at Alexandra, came and took the chair opposite her.

She didn't meet his eyes. "You must love her very much," she said, her tone strangled.

At first Drew looked puzzled by the statement. "Do you mean Genevieve? Isn't that quite obvious?"

Her eyes went to the silver-framed photo of Emily on the mantel. "I meant her," she said.

His eyes went there, too, and his face softened. "I did," he said, simply. "I loved her very much."

She noticed he used the past tense.

"I think of her every day—Genevieve reminds me of her every day."

For a moment they were both quiet, sipping their hot chocolate. Then he spoke again.

"You know, I never wanted weddings here because I felt as if it would be a betrayal of Emily. That was her dream. Our dream together. And yet, now that it's happening, I feel completely differently about it. It's not a betrayal of her. It's a way of honoring what mattered to her. I know that Ivy and Sebastian's wedding here is going to be everything she ever hoped a wedding at Parker and Parker could ever be."

No pressure there, Alexandra thought.

"And now," Drew said softly, "I feel the same way about you as I felt about the weddings."

She was so surprised she burned her mouth on the rim of the mug. She set it down hastily.

"It's not a betrayal of Emily," he continued, "to see another woman. To start living again. For the longest time, just like with the weddings, I felt it would be. But now I see saying yes to life is a way of honoring her. It's honoring everything she stood for. She believed in love more than any other thing."

"Love?" Alexandra squeaked.

He looked slightly abashed. "I don't know if it's going to go there, Alexandra. That's why I wanted to take our time."

Our time, she thought, as in her and him together. As if somehow, suddenly, time belonged to both of them. She felt almost dizzy from the shock of what he was saying.

"That's why I wanted to slow everything down," he continued, his voice so soft, so serious.

So sexy.

"That's why I said I wanted to get to know you first."

"First?"

"Passion confuses everything."

You don't say, she thought, her heart racing.

"Not that the passion isn't there. I mean, it's more than obvious, isn't it?"

She nodded, unable to speak. The scent of him on the clothing she was wearing seemed to intensify. She was way too aware that the cloth on her skin had touched his skin not so long ago. In combination with his words, it was a strangely intense intimacy.

"But I want to be the man Emily would have expected me to be. I want to be the kind of man I would hope for for my daughter."

"Oh," she said. Her voice came out a strangled croak.

"I know it's old-fashioned, maybe hopelessly

so, but I want us both to be sure what's happening between us is as strong and as real as it seems in this moment."

Alexandra started to laugh.

His brows lowered. "I'm sorry. I'm kind of making a declaration here. I don't see what's so funny."

The laughter was hard to bite back. It was as if there was a well of joy inside her, and it was bubbling over.

"Drew, when you told me you wanted to slow down and get to know each other, I thought it was a variation of *I really like you, but let's just be friends.*"

The tiniest smile played across the beautiful line of his mouth.

"I thought," she continued, "it was like, *Let's have a platonic relationship.*"

"Forever?" he said, so obviously appalled at the idea that she laughed again.

"That's what I thought."

"Huh," he said. "Clearly I suck at wooing a woman in the same way I suck at making Christmas for a little girl."

"Wooing a woman?"

"I'm being old-fashioned again. That was a stupid choice of phrase. Sheesh. It's not like I keep a stack of old gothic novels under my bed."

The fact that he—the man who had everything, the man who was so successful and so sophisticated—was so awkward and so uncomfortable totally enchanted her.

"So, just for clarity," Alexandra said, still feeling laughter gurgling inside her, "you're proposing to romance me?"

"Exactly," he said, looking deeply relieved that she had gotten it. "And just for the record, I think having a platonic relationship with you *forever* would be impossible."

"Oh," she said, suddenly serious, that gurgling laughter dying abruptly. She swallowed.

"So, as far as dates go, the first two probably sucked."

"We've had two dates?" she said.

"See? I told you I sucked. You didn't even know. Well, who can blame you? For the first one, last night, I was a horse's ass—"

"Not just the ass," she clarified, and there was the laughter again, a well that would not be capped.

"And for the second one, the building of snowmen, I failed to impress with a feat of strength."

"I think, actually, it might be *three* dates," she said, getting into this lovely spirit of teasing. "If we count the Rockingbird cocktail night."

"See? I'm in hopelessly over my head."

"Well, we did kiss," she reminded him. "So I think it qualifies."

His eyes moved to her lips, his expression smoky with remembrance.

CHAPTER FIFTEEN

"I'M COUNTING ON you to be the expert on romance," Drew told Alexandra. Was he still looking at her lips?

She had a feeling of wanting to pinch herself. Drew Parker wanted to have a romance. With her.

"Me?" she said. "The expert?"

"Wedding planner?"

"Oh, that." She blushed. "It's not really what people think. It's a lot of hard work and basic business. It's having an eye for detail—being a perfectionist, really—and having superb organizational skills."

"I see," he said. "Kind of like being the librarian of the wedding world."

She was making herself sound dull! Or as if she was reciting her résumé.

"Well, not quite like that."

"Oh," he said, as if he was disappointed. Good grief. Did every man have a librarian fantasy? She thought of his fingers pulling that braid from her hair last night, and shivered more than she had when she had gotten snow soaked.

"Not that there isn't an artistic side to it. Not that I don't use imagination, and often…" Now she was chattering.

"I've seen your website."

"You have?"

He looked a little embarrassed. "I had a little peek after we first met. It looked pretty romantic to me. From a male perspective, frighteningly so."

"Oh. I mean, being able to infuse a single day with a sense of romantic bliss is not really the same as conducting a romance, uh…day to day. Personally. I think you're probably far more an expert than me."

"Me? The expert?" He looked terrified. It was adorable.

"Well," Alexandra told him, "you've actually had a successful relationship. You must have been romantic with Emily. It sounds as if she loved romance. Look at this place. Look at the dream she had for it."

He considered that, and then in a low tone, like a man giving a confession, he said, "I'm afraid Em's love of romance made me quite lazy in that department. She came up with ideas, I went along. Happily. But I'll confess to never having an original romantic idea in my life."

"Well, you didn't get so lucky this time. Except for the fact I plan weddings, I really haven't gotten out much." The way he was looking at her lips was making her think, *Romance equals kisses. Lots and lots of kisses.*

He smiled at her. "Alexandra Harris?"

"Yes?"

"Would you like to conduct a romance with me?"

He was annoyed with himself. How had he managed to make that sound like a science experiment? And yet, the look Alexandra gave him, Drew realized, could only be described as radiant.

She was in his house, on his couch, in his clothes, looking radiant. He hadn't really seen this coming when she had rescued his daughter just about a month ago. He thought he had protected himself from unexpected turns in the road of life.

"Yes," she said softly, tentatively, almost shyly. "Yes, I would. I'd like to conduct a romance with you."

Her sweet tone made him quite glad that somehow she had sneaked by all his defenses. But then it struck him that all that radiance was a huge responsibility. What if he let her down? But wasn't that the whole point of going slow? Building in safeguards. Against broken expectations. And broken hearts. Revealing to her slowly how flawed he was.

What if he broke her heart? What if she broke his? It was a little late for doubt. He'd already asked her if she wanted to conduct a romance. She'd already said yes.

He felt a little thrill, even though it was apparent neither of them knew the first thing about it.

"So," he said, feeling his way, "maybe we should go on a date. Luckily, we've gotten the first two—possibly three—dates out of the way. They can be notoriously awkward."

"Notoriously," she agreed with a smile. Was she looking at his lips? It was going to be hard to keep this on the straight and narrow if she kept looking at him like that.

"What would you like to do for our next date?" he said.

There was that look again, smoldering. Her eyes said, *I know exactly what I want to do.* Out loud, she said, "I don't know."

"Tell me what your perfect fourth date would be," he insisted, "Hopefully, something better than the first three."

"I thought the first three were just fine," she said.

"Hardly romantic."

"But definitely fun. And I don't know, Rockingbird night was a bit romantic. And you did end up at my place last night. Undressed. And I'm here today. Also undressed."

She laughed, and in her laughter he heard that nothing was ever going to quite go as planned with her. For a guy with control issues, that should have been terrifying. Instead if felt exhilarating.

"But let's step up our game," he suggested. "What would be the perfect romantic date for you?"

"You tell me first."

The silence stretched between them.

"I have an idea," Drew finally said. "Let's both write down three ideas for a perfect date and we'll pull them out of a hat, one at a time, until we've done them all."

And he was thinking, *at the end of six dates, we'll know.* Which felt faintly ridiculous, because watching her, her bare feet tucked under her, in his pajamas and his T-shirt, her hair cascading over her shoulder and absorbing the light of the fire as if it had flame sewn into the strands, it felt as if he already knew.

Slow, he warned himself. He reached into a drawer on a side table and pulled out a paper pad. He ripped off a piece and kept it for himself, then handed her the pad and a pen.

"You're getting the hang of this," she said, taking the pad of paper from him, "because *that's* romantic. Three ideas each for the perfect date."

Honestly, the look she gave him was as if he had written her a love sonnet.

"Let's make the ideas just about us," he said. "No Genevieve."

He wanted to tell himself it was to protect his

daughter, just in case there was a heartache hidden in there somewhere.

But the truth was he wanted the intensity of alone time. Just the grown-ups.

"But I wanted to make cookies with her! Christmas cookies."

"It's a bit early for that. Christmas, that is, not cookie making."

"According to Genevieve, it's Christmas right now."

"Well, until the snow melts. Don't get me wrong, I'm all for cookie making, Christmas or otherwise, but for a *romantic* date? No."

She looked down at her paper, her tongue caught between her teeth in the most delectable way. She chewed on the top of the pen.

He looked down at his own paper. He had a vision of looking at her through steam, across a bathtub filled with hot water, candles surrounding it and rose petals floating on top. Would renting a place with an outdoor hot tub be too risqué?

Way too risqué. And risky, given his honorable intentions. He wouldn't look at her.

He wrote down *Candlelit dinner.* He was quite pleased with himself. He had managed to include candles in a non-X-rated way. He glanced at her. Now she was smiling slightly as she looked down at her paper. Her pen moved across it.

He wrote *movie.* Then he crossed it out. He checked his phone to see what was popular on

Broadway right now. He wrote that down. He frowned. Would that be two dates? One, out for dinner, and two, live theater? Wouldn't it be more romantic if it was one?

Way more romantic if it was one. Should he name a restaurant? It should be exclusive and expensive. A special-occasion kind of restaurant.

This seemed to be getting complicated, but he wrote down the name of a restaurant he had enjoyed with a business acquaintance and the name of a play that was popular.

But that meant he still had to come up with two more dates. He was beginning to think this had been quite a dumb idea.

He wrote down *National Hockey League game at Madison Square Garden*. He glared at it. Obviously, that would be perfect for *him*.

Dating a woman like Alexandra Harris required him to be a better man. He needed to think about what she would like. He glanced at her. He scratched out the hockey idea and wrote, *Carriage ride in Central Park*.

Central Park! Skating. It was a little early for that, though. Despite today's unexpected snowfall, the Conservatory Water wasn't frozen yet. And actually, the rinks didn't seem as if they would be any more romantic than bringing her to a hockey game.

Was he sweating?

He glanced over at her. She looked as if she was having fun!

He looked down at his paper. *Think.*

He saw a vision of them, sitting on this couch, a fire in the hearth, covered in a blanket, a bowl of popcorn between them, a movie on the flat screen that was revealed when he pushed a button and the picture covering it rolled away.

But they'd already done that. At her place. He wanted to be original. And spectacular.

She was done. She had been for some time. And she was watching him with amusement. He felt faintly panicky. In a rush of desperation, he wrote down *Lunch and wine in a hot air balloon.*

He didn't even know if such things happened in the wintertime. It would probably be cold. And uncomfortable.

"Done?" she asked.

"Sure," he said. He could work out the logistics later. They could go to California. Hot air balloons probably ran there year-round, if they didn't run here. She could come with him and Genevieve.

Though, the truth was, California was feeling less attractive by the minute. Things were not getting any better for Gabe, so it was possible they wouldn't be going to California and maybe the hot air balloon would have to be postponed...

He was making it too complicated. He left the hot air balloon suggestion. He tore his piece of paper into three, and with no hat in sight, dumped them in a bowl beside him. He crossed over to her and held out the bowl. She put her scraps of paper in.

"Be careful with that," she said. "I think it's Ming."

"It's okay. Pick one."

"You pick one," she said.

"Okay." He closed his eyes, reached into the bowl and shuffled through the papers with his fingertips. He drew one out.

He stared at it. *Hot tub under the stars.* He frowned. Hadn't he written that down and then scratched it out? He realized it wasn't his handwriting.

"Uh…" he said, crumpling the paper in his hand, and shoving it deep in his pocket. "Hockey game at Madison Square Garden."

The exercise had been to select an activity that was romantic, he reminded himself. A hockey game was something he and Gabe might do. He'd already eliminated it, so why had he blurted that out?

Obviously pure panic had set in. He had needed to escape from an evening in a hot tub. With her. That was a test he just wasn't ready for. Would she be a one-piece gal? Or two-piece? Or maybe—

How did a man keep his decency about him in the face of all this temptation? Yes, hockey was a good choice. A safe choice. A surrounded-by-a-zillion-people choice. A something-to-focus-on-other-than-her-lips choice.

Still, had he disappointed her?

She didn't look disappointed. "I've never been to a live hockey game before. I think it will be fun."

He squinted at her to see if she was being sincere. He had the feeling she didn't know how to be anything else.

Unlike him, who was willing to fudge the results of a simple draw. For the best of reasons, though. To protect them *both*.

"Even though I've never been to a live game, I do love the Rangers," she said.

He figured it was pretty much hopeless to protect himself from a woman who loved the Rangers. And she wasn't just saying that, either, because she knew Madison Square Garden meant the Rangers, not the Islanders or the Devils.

"My brother is going to be so jealous," she said gleefully.

He needed to remember that. It should keep him on the straight and honorable path. She had a brother, who, if he was not mistaken, while telling Alexandra that she was thirty-one and it was none of his business what she did, had shot Drew a not-very-subtle warning look this morning.

Don't hurt my sister.

Drew looked up the game schedule on his phone. "Are you free next Thursday?"

"Thursday is perfect. Most of my weddings are

on Saturdays, so Saturday is out for me, right up until Christmas."

Christmas, he thought. If he didn't manage to blow this, they would still be together at Christmas. She seemed to have an expectation they would still be dating at Christmas.

Which meant two people would have expectations of him. What did you get someone you were dating for Christmas?

"Friday is always a crazy day," she said. Apparently the mere mention of Christmas had not sent her into a cold sweat. "Last-minute details. Who are they playing?"

Who was who playing? Oh, the Rangers. There was no sense getting ahead of himself. He could just take this one date at a time.

"Um," he looked back to his phone. "Boston."

He was going away for Christmas.

But just like that, he knew wasn't. Gabe wasn't going to be back at work by then, though that had the feeling of an excuse. Drew remembered Alexandra had mentioned baking Christmas cookies. California and all its manufactured cheer suddenly seemed to dull in the light of making Christmas cookies.

Of getting ready for Christmas with her.

He felt something in him relax. With her, he didn't think it would be about meeting her expectations: the perfect gift, the great tree, the right feeling.

With her it would be about sharing both the stresses and joys of the season.

The last thing he had expected when he'd suggested they try conducting a romance was this. It had been a long, long time since he had felt this way.

Not alone.

CHAPTER SIXTEEN

THE ARENA ERUPTED in a cheer that deepened to a deafening roar as the New York Rangers scored the winning goal in the second minute of overtime.

Alexandra leaped to her feet and screamed until she was hoarse, just like everybody else. She became aware Drew was looking at her, smiling.

He looked so wonderful, his face alight with the excitement of the game, casual in a sports jacket, a button-down shirt, jeans. He was wearing a plaid scarf tucked loosely under the lapels of the jacket. It wasn't the one he had put on the snowman, because she had returned to get that one, and it was now wrapped around the neck of the stuffed frog he had won for her on Halloween.

So few men wore scarves well. He was definitely one of them. They had on the matching ball caps Drew had bought for them from a vendor in the lobby. She had put hers on and then turned it backward.

"I like it," he'd said, regarding her with laughter-filled eyes. "The sexy tomboy look."

She had told her brother where she was going and borrowed his treasured Rangers jersey for the occasion.

He wouldn't surrender it until she texted Drew and asked him where the seats were.

Then he had handed it over willingly, with a little whistle under his breath.

"A Rangers game," Shaun said. "At the blue line, second level, first row. So much better than ice level. This guy knows what he's doing. He's a keeper—you know that, right?"

The jersey wasn't really sexy—it was way too big—but when she saw how Drew's eyes lit up when she'd met him outside the Garden, she knew there were things more important than being sexy.

He had kissed her on the cheek in greeting, and she had known her brother was right on all counts. Drew knew what he was doing. He was a keeper.

They both had to work in the morning—she had an extra-challenging wedding coming up over the weekend—so they reluctantly parted ways after the game. He touched his lips to hers, a mere brush, but long after he had put her in a car, the excitement of the evening shimmered inside her. It felt as if her tummy was full of butterflies.

It felt exactly the way it was supposed to feel.
And had never felt before.

It felt—terrifyingly and exhilaratingly—as if she was falling off a cliff, waiting to see if she would crash or if she would fly.

Her phone buzzed with his ringtone.

"Hey," she said.

"I'm at home."

"I'm not quite, yet."

"I've got the bowl in front of me. Should I pick the next one?"

"You have to pick it blind."

"I know the rules!"

She closed her eyes as she heard him rustling through the papers. She knew which one she wanted.

The dangerous one. A night in a hot tub under the stars.

"Huh," he said. "This is one of yours."

She could feel herself crossing her fingers... and her toes. Like a gambler begging for the perfect numbers, please, please, please...

"A dance lesson?" he said. "Alexandra, have mercy."

"It will be fun," she said. Not as much fun as a hot tub, but still—

"I'm a terrible dancer."

"Me, too!"

"Then why torture us?"

"It's important to stretch," she said.

"Let's switch it out for a yoga class then!"

Why had she chosen a dance class? First of all, she'd been trying to think fast. But secondly, more and more weddings featured a dance sequence the bride and groom worked on for weeks—sometimes months—before the wedding. She could see a difference in couples after even the first lesson: a subtle deepening of the connection and laughter between them.

She often had couples tell her that turned out to be their favorite memory of the day.

"As tempting as it is to see you in downward-facing dog, I don't think we should start changing the rules." Because what would that mean when the hot tub came up?

He sighed dramatically. "I take it you'll line this up?"

"I have contacts," she said. "I'll be in touch."

"Soon?" he whispered. Even with his reluctance to take a dance class, he was eager to see her again, soon.

"Soon," she whispered. As she disconnected, that feeling of leaping off the cliff intensified.

The next day at work, her assistant kept giving her sideways looks.

"What is going on with you?" she finally asked. "New vitamins? An exercise program? You look so—"

"What?" Alexandra squeaked.

Her assistant regarded her thoughtfully and then smiled. "You look like one of our new brides, just flushed with love. Alexandra! Are you in love?"

"Don't be silly," she said hastily, even as she felt the shock of that question. She realized why the sensation of falling was so strong. She was falling, all right—she was falling in love.

Even though she knew it took some of her couples many sessions to learn a dance sequence for their weddings, Alexandra soon realized her expectations of the one-hour dance date had been unrealistic.

As it turned out, along with her own lack of skill, Drew had two left feet. And a personality conflict with the teacher, Claudia, who had all the charm of a drill instructor. In a whisper, Drew dubbed the instructor Clattila the Bun because of her attitude and the way her hair was so severely pulled back.

"Man hater," he whispered in Alexandra's ear, as he was finally allowed to take her hand after they had practiced a box step by themselves, mirroring the instructor, for a painfully long time.

Clattila the Bun shouted out the cadence.

"One, two, three…no, no, no, Mr. Parker. Hips, hips. Argh! Let me show you *again*. You—" she pointed at Alexandra "—stand over there."

She shoved Alexandra out of the way and took Drew's hand. Over the instructor's shoulder, Drew shuffled along with deliberate clumsiness and made faces at Alexandra that dissolved her into giggles.

When they moved close to her, he muttered to Alexandra, "I thought nobody put Baby in the corner?"

Then he took charge. He put his cheek to the instructor's, executed an about turn, shot their arms out like arrows from their shoulders and practically dragged her in the opposite direction, across the room.

"You are not taking this seriously, Mr. Parker!"

He glanced over his shoulder and lifted a fiendishly uncooperative eyebrow at Alexandra. He let go of the instructor, ran across the highly polished floor, fell to his knees and slid to Alexandra, his arms spread wide.

Unfortunately, Drew's pants weren't quite up to the strain put on them by the move. They tore open with a loud ripping sound.

Alexandra laughed so hard she doubled over from it. If she wasn't such a good customer, she was fairly certain they might have been kicked out of class, but to the obvious relief of the instructor, Drew, with a comically regretful look at the damage to his pants, voluntarily withdrew.

With his jacket tied around his waist, standing outside the studio, they called a car.

"Thanks for trying to rescue that," Alexandra said, the laughter still trying to bubble to the surface. "I did hope it would be a little more like an '80s musical. You would have made an awesome Catskills summer resort dance instructor, by the way. A born rebel."

As he held open the car door for her, he grinned that wicked bad-boy smile that sent her stomach spinning down to her toes. She slid past him and sank into a luxurious leather seat.

"To be honest," he said, getting in beside her, "when you said dance class, I had hoped for a little more maraca shaking myself. Clattila suspected. That's why she hated me. And yet still?"

He wagged mischievous eyebrows at Alexandra. His eyes looked as green as a cool pond on a hot summer afternoon. Awareness of him tickled along her spine in the way she had hoped it would when she had suggested a dance class as a date idea.

"Still, I'm having the time of my life." And then he hummed a few bars of a familiar song. He took her hand. After a moment, she hummed, too.

He started to sing. And then she sang along. She'd always thought it was dumb when people burst into song in musicals, but it didn't feel dumb at all. It felt joyous and connected and funny and lovely.

It was true. Here they were sitting in a car, all the life and bustle of New York unfolding outside the windows, as they enjoyed their own private world and sang the same song. She *was* having the time of her life.

The car pulled up at Parker and Parker.

"Should I ask the driver to take you home or are you coming in? I don't think it made the list of romantic dates, but I heard you can have a mean game of Candy Land here."

Alexandra considered the invitation. She had so much work to do. And yet, it was irresistible. Genevieve and Lila greeted them both with such enthusiasm, especially when Candy Land was mentioned. They eagerly hauled out the game while Drew went and changed his pants. They set up at a table in the playroom that was much too small for everyone but Genevieve.

"I just remembered why I hate this game," Drew said later. "No skill, no choice. Just follow the directions. And mine say I have to go back three squares."

Genevieve chortled. "You're going to lose, Daddy."

He made a face, and all of them dissolved into giggles. After that he had them howling as he tried on different facial expressions to express dismay and glee over the game.

"As tempting as it is to while away my life playing Candy Land," Alexandra finally said, noticing the room had gotten quite dark, "I'd better go."

Drew got to his feet and winced from being in such a cramped position so long.

"Before you go, let's pick our next great date out of the bowl."

They went downstairs, and he held it out for her. She peered at it, hoping she might see a little ink bleed-through that would let her know which one was the hot tub one.

He noticed and held the bowl over his head.

She stood on her tippy-toes and reached into it. She held her breath. She opened the folded paper. "Cook a new recipe together," she read and felt the stab of disappointment. Really? She was ready for something steamier, figuratively and literally!

"That must be your idea. I don't cook. I hope it doesn't involve lessons."

She laughed. "Of course it doesn't involve lessons. I thought we could do it at my place. Even though the kitchen is tiny, I know where everything is."

Or was it because that tiny kitchen gave them much more opportunity to bump into each other than his rather large one?

"We just have to pick a recipe neither of us has made before," she told him.

"Well, that's easy for me."

She thought of her schedule. She wished she had picked something else out of their dating bowl. Because she had been thinking about what they could make together ever since she had written down the idea and put it in that bowl. The recipes she had narrowed it down to—beef Wellington, baked Alaska—required quite a big commitment in time, and so it meant she wouldn't see him for a week.

"How about next Sunday, my place?" she asked.

"I don't want to wait that long," he growled. She shivered. They were more and more on the same wavelength.

"But when I wrote it down," she said, stubbornly, "I was thinking about a meal that was complex."

"Like a great book," he said. "Like a good wine."

"Exactly," she said. "Layers of discovery."

"Every time you open it, you notice something new. A texture, a nuance, a secret that wasn't apparent at first. Like you."

He was being a flirt. And she loved it.

"I did want the cooking challenge to be difficult," Alexandra told him, trying to stay on track. "Not a workaday meal. Something that requires a stretch."

"Stretching again! I'm sure, subconsciously, what you really want is to see me in yoga class. You probably want to see my pants rip again."

She did want to see his pants ripped again. Off. By her. Alexandra was shocked by the thought. She made herself talk about their next date.

"What I hoped for was a sense of a mission completed together."

Heads bent over the cookbook. Hands accidentally touching. Bumping into him on the way to the fridge. Lips tasting off the same spoon.

"A recipe that's hard," she went on. "That requires teamwork. That requires us to see how we work with one another."

"If we cooked a dish that was a little simpler, I could ask Lila to stay late Tuesday night," he said.

"Hot dogs it is," she said. "See you Tuesday. My place."

He grinned at her. "See? We've just demonstrated how well we work together."

And then he kissed her goodbye and demonstrated that things did not need to be any more complex between them than they already were.

CHAPTER SEVENTEEN

THE FIRST TEXT arrived from Drew at 9:00 a.m. Tuesday morning while Alexandra was working with her assistant on Ivy and Sebastian's wedding. Her first thought, when she saw it was him, was that he was going to cancel.

And so, when she read the text, her heart stood still.

I have a confession to make.

A thousand possibilities raced through her mind.
There's someone else.
I can't get over my wife after all.

Oh?

I said we worked well together, but I wasn't being totally honest.

Damn. Damn. Damn.

Oh?

I don't really like hot dogs.

She laughed out loud, mostly relieved, partly delighted at his teasing. Her assistant shot her a look.

Smokies?

What's a smoky?

A kind of sausage. There's different flavors. The cheese-stuffed ones are good.

I do like a girl who knows her sausages. Do you prefer big or little sausages?

She chortled. She blushed.

Her assistant muttered, "I knew it."

After that little exchange, Alexandra thought she should shut off her phone, and yet somehow the more they went back and forth, the more her creativity was fed and the better her ideas for Sebastian and Ivy's wedding became. It seemed as if she was infusing it with an element of fun—and even sexiness—that she had never had quite like this in a wedding before.

They ended up deciding on homemade pizza. Had a grocery store ever felt quite so dazzling as it did when she was selecting ingredients, and just the right wine, to share with Drew?

There was no awkwardness when he arrived. There was just a sense—she hoped in both of them—of this being where they belonged.

Together.

Her kitchen was so small that there was lots of bumping into each other. Plenty of hand touching. Much tasting of ingredients off the same spoon. There was laughter threaded through with a lovely tension, a sizzling awareness of each other, as the conversation flowed freely.

He made her laugh with a story about Genevieve. But then, when he updated her about Gabe and his mom, it was just as easy to be serious with him as it was to laugh.

She told him about the bridezilla of last weekend's wedding and gave him the latest changes to Ivy and Sebastian's wedding details that she had made that day.

An unspoken anticipation was building as they headed toward the inevitable. They were both aware that yet another layer of this relationship was calling to them, crooning to them, begging for their discovery.

And yet, Alexandra was aware of wanting to not rush this part, either. Because once they let the other out—once they opened the door on all the passion that shimmered and sparked in the air between them—it would become everything.

It would be all encompassing. It would swallow up everything else.

No, it would be wise to wait, to hold that change at bay. Then, if it did go somewhere else—and she felt no doubt that it would, once the hot tub date came up—they would know each other completely on so many other levels first.

The pizza was dreadful: the crust burned on the edges and doughy in the middle. Neither of them noticed.

"Of all the dates so far," Drew said, lying on the couch, his head propped up in her lap, eating ice cream from a bowl, "this is my favorite."

"Even though there was no beef Wellington?"

"We'll save that for a different time," he said.

A different time. A future beyond the dwindling date ideas they had both put in that bowl.

They had known each other just about six weeks. And already it was becoming difficult to picture a life without him in it.

He stayed too late for a work night. She had no regrets and found that when he was at the door, bundling up against a very cold November night, she didn't want him to go.

"I took the liberty of picking our next item out of the bowl. I didn't look, though. A surprise for both of us."

He handed her the slip of paper. Again, she felt herself wishing. Even though she knew this wasn't wise, she was aware of feeling *ready* for what came next.

Maybe even beginning to need what came next.

She unfolded the paper and read it and tried not to look too crestfallen. It was delightful, after all. Dinner and live theater. He'd even picked the restaurant and the play. Both had been on her list of *want to* for some time.

And after this, there would be only two more things. They were drawing ever closer to investigating the sensuality that was in the background of everything they did. Maybe, she thought whimsically, a force greater than her was saving the best for last.

"Do you want to do it tomorrow?" he asked.

She laughed. "Won't it be hard to get reservations and tickets on such short notice?"

"Where there's a will, there's a way."

It made her tingle that he felt exactly the same way as her. As if they could not get enough of each other.

Not ever.

And so the next night, drunk on each other's company, Alexandra and Drew had the most perfect New York City evening. They had an exquisite dinner. They saw a play that was funny and well done.

As they walked, hand in hand, through the park, back to his place, breathing in the clouds of each other's breath, Alexandra realized she had joined a club that she had always felt excluded from.

She was part of a couple.

When they arrived at his place, Lila had not been successful in getting Genevieve to bed, and she looked exhausted.

"I'll take care of it," Alexandra said, and she felt the most heart-warming sense of homecoming as Genevieve took her hand and they went up to her room.

Soon, the little girl was in bed, a favorite storybook out. Drew saw Lila home and then came and joined them. Alexandra scooted over, all three of them in the bed.

She had felt like part of a couple earlier, but the magic deepened as Drew took the book from her and read it, his voice deep and soothing.

She felt like part of a family. Genevieve sagged against her, fast asleep in seconds. Alexandra and Drew tiptoed from the room.

"Let's pull from the bowl before you go," he said.

Again, she felt exhilarated, the anticipation building. And again, she felt disappointed as she read the paper.

That was crazy! Who could possibly feel disappointed that the man she was falling in love with had come up with such an incredibly romantic idea?

"A hot air balloon ride," she read. "With wine.

And lunch. Um… Drew, it's November. Do they go in November?"

"I wondered the same thing. So I checked."

Just like she had been checking. She had spent way too much time dreamily looking up where one went to spend an evening in a hot tub under the stars in New York. And how fitting was it that that would be the final occasion they pulled from the bowl?

"And yes, hot air balloons go all year round. Over the Hudson Valley."

"It sounds slightly terrifying," she said.

"I know," he agreed. "That's the best part, isn't it?"

She looked at him. She was aware his face had become so familiar to her. Drew Parker did not even seem like the same man she had first laid eyes on weeks ago.

He didn't seem formidable at all. The darkness seemed to have been chased from him; his eyes danced with light. His smile was playful.

She couldn't help it.

She stood on her tiptoes and put her hand on his neck and drew Drew's lips down to her own.

"Wow," he said, pulling away from her after a long time. "If terrifying is the best part, I don't think we have to go on a balloon ride."

But they did go on a hot air balloon ride. It wasn't terrifying. Not even a little bit. It was absolutely exhilarating, and surprisingly warm, as they caught the morning updraft. Drifting with the wind gave the illusion of there being no wind at all. And the balloon, after all, was fueled by a propane heater that allowed them to feel toasty warm even as it provided lift.

The morning had been frosty, and as Alexandra looked down at the world from the great height of the balloon, everything was gilded in silver. The fields, the trees, the doll-like barns and houses, were all sparkling.

And Drew stood behind her, his arms wrapped around her waist, and she leaned into the now familiar strength of him.

Alexandra allowed herself to relax against him, to feel the magic of the moment deeply. What a wonderful world it was that an ordinary woman like her could have an extraordinary moment like this.

He gently turned her away from the view so that she faced him. She looked at him with complete wonder. How had this happened? Her ordinary life transformed into an absolute fairy tale. And this man: so funny, so smart, so handsome, her perfect prince.

Indeed, she felt like a princess, as if she had been asleep for a long, long time.

She knew what would wake her up. And so did he. With their hearts soaring as high as that hot air balloon, their lips touched, held, tangled.

And just like the princess in every fairy tale, Alexandra was awoken by a kiss.

The sensation of soaring lasted in Drew long after the balloon had landed. It had nothing to do with the champagne they had sipped and everything to do with her lips.

Not just her lips. *Her.* Her hand in his. Her eyes on his face. Her sense of wonder. The way she saw the world. Her laughter. The way she made him laugh. The ease of being together. The tension that sizzled tantalizingly between them.

He had told himself he would *know* at the end of six dates, but he knew now.

"I know what the last date is," she told him softly when the balloon had landed. "I wrote it."

"I know what it is, too."

"What? You cheated? You looked?"

"Confession time. I picked it first."

She stared at him. If he'd expected annoyance or anger, he was surprised. She laughed, delighted.

Alexandra, he realized, would be a constant surprise to him. Even if they were together thirty years from now. Forty. Fifty. Even when Genevieve was all grown-up and they were bouncing their grandchildren on their knees.

He felt something go very still in him.

"But there were six pieces of paper in there," she said.

"I made up the hockey game on the spot and put the hot tub suggestion in my pocket. The one left is a carriage ride in Central Park."

"A carriage ride?" Her breath was frosty in the air. "I've always wanted to do that. Funny how you can live in a place like New York City your whole life and not avail yourself to what it offers."

As she spoke, he *knew*. It was the sound of her voice and the light in her eyes; it was the puffiness of her just-kissed lips and her willingness to explore the whole world with him, to make even the familiar seem new and shiny.

He knew he wanted to spend the rest of his life with her.

"Drew?" She reached up and touched his face. Her hands were encased in angora mittens. Her touch, even through the mittens, felt as if it could melt him.

He wanted to blurt it out, right here, right now. *I love you. Marry me.*

But it was a bit like making Christmas for a child. It was an occasion he wanted to be memorable. He wanted to be the better man. He didn't want his marriage proposal to be about meeting some need in him, but about making wishes—that she might not even know she still held deep in her heart—come true.

He wanted romance. He wanted fireworks.

He wanted Alexandra to think back on that

moment for the rest of her life with joy and re-membered bliss.

"I looked it up," she admitted, her shyness en-dearing. "There's a lovely inn in the Catskills that has a hot tub. A pool, really. It's like a se-cret grotto."

She was blushing.

"You've given this some thought," he teased her.

Her blush deepened. A lifetime of making her blush...

But then Drew had the horrible thought that at the inn in the Catskills, as lovely as it might be, not everything would be in his control. What if it wasn't completely private? What if someone else was using it at the same time? What if they were interrupted? What if the pool and the rooms didn't look as good—as was so often the case—as the pictures showed?

"Not that I have time to go to the Catskills right now," she said, suddenly uneasy. She was reading his silence as reluctance. "December is always such a frantically busy month. Ivy and Sebas-tian's wedding is around the corner. And all the nieces and nephews have Christmas concerts."

How could you not love a person who gave their nieces' and nephews' Christmas concerts the same priority as the wedding of the century?

"How about if we plan our last date—" *and the first day of the rest of our lives* "—for the day after Ivy and Sebastian's wedding?" he said. "And how about if I look after all the details?"

She looked at him, her eyes huge, her lower lip trembling. He was aware he was holding his breath, waiting for her answer.

It was the next stage unfolding. And it was momentous. She knew it. And he knew it.

"Yes," Alexandra said.

CHAPTER EIGHTEEN

ALEXANDRA HAD BEEN RIGHT, Drew thought. December was a frantically busy month. He had just come out from the banquet hall of Parker and Parker—almost ready for the big day—and been led by laughter, and the smell of baking, to the kitchen in his house.

Genevieve and Alexandra were giggling over cookies, laid out, individually, on one side of the long kitchen island. It looked as if there were, easily, a hundred cookies there. They were golden around the edges and shaped like stars and trees and Christmas ornaments.

At the other end of the enormous island were stacks of brand-new backpacks, the tags still on them.

He wandered in. "What is all this?"

The kitchen was a disaster of open cupboard doors, leaning bags of ingredients, used bowls and spilled flour. Sprinkles crunched under his feet. The space had never seemed more welcoming.

Genevieve was standing on a chair. Her hair was pulled back in a ponytail, and she had on a pinafore apron. She had confectioners' sugar on the tip of her nose, and she had found a place on the dress not protected by the apron and managed to get a green food coloring stain on it. She had a piping bag in her hand and, if he was not mistaken, there were sprinkles in her hair. Her lips were the same color as the icing in the piping bag.

"We're making cookies for Mr. Evans and his mom."

"That's a lot of cookies for Gabe and his mom." Drew sidled over. "I guess I can have one?"

He reached, and Alexandra smacked his hand lightly with a wooden spoon. He yelped loudly, put his knuckles to his mouth, and while she went wide-eyed, wondering if she had hit him too hard, he snaked out his other hand, grabbed a cookie and stuffed the whole thing in his mouth.

"Delicious," he proclaimed.

"Daddy, we need them all!" Genevieve nodded toward the backpacks. "For those. We're putting other things in, too. Socks and toothbrushes. And what else, Alex?"

"Um… Books. Scarves. Soap. Toothpaste."

His house had become this: chaos, laughter, energy.

His life had become this place: going to see the tree lit up at Rockefeller Center, Christmas concerts, sledding on Pilgrim Hill, skating on the now-frozen Conservatory Water.

His work had become this: helping get Parker and Parker ready for Ivy and Sebastian's wedding.

Though his input, as far as the wedding went, was completely unnecessary.

He'd seen that right away. That Alexandra had an extraordinarily talented and skilled team. She was a magic maker and an enchantress.

And yet when she was over there working, so close to him, Drew found he could not *not* be there. Seeing her at work and in her element revealed yet another facet of her, as sparkling and deep as the facets on a diamond.

And then, once he'd been there, he'd made a suggestion. And then another one. And then he'd been part of that team, fully engrossed in working toward someone else's perfect day.

But it wasn't just a day. He could see that in the way Alexandra worked on it. For her it was keeping a promise.

She had promised this couple a wondrous beginning. Magical. Beautiful beyond their wildest imaginings.

And Drew was shocked by how much he loved being part of her vision for Ivy and Sebastian.

He was delighted by how well they worked together. Reading each other's thoughts, on the same wavelength, sharing similar tastes. They were such an extraordinary team.

It solidified the commitment he was going to make to her the day after that wedding. In a setting as romantic as he could make it—at least as romantic as these settings she created, which set the bar high—he was going to ask her to share the rest of his life with him.

To be a mother to his daughter. And maybe, someday, other babies, too. He could see now, as he had seen dozens of times over the last weeks, with Alexandra's head bent over what seemed to be hundreds of cookies, exactly what a good mother she was going to be.

Wife.

He felt a shiver of pure anticipation for all the things that word meant. Of course, she still had to say yes.

"How come you're filling these backpacks?" he asked. "Who are they for?"

"They're for homeless people," Genevieve said, her face lit as she bent over her task. She deposited quite a large blob of red icing on one of the cookies. She regarded it for a moment, picked up her shaker of green sprinkles and doused it.

"I think you missed a spot," he teased her.

She regarded her cookie. "I didn't. Did I, Alexandra?"

She moved closer to the little girl, rested her hand lightly on her shoulder, regarded the cookie in question solemnly.

"I think it's perfect."

Genevieve beamed. "We're buying toys, too. For the kids at the shelter. Daddy, did you know there are kids that don't get presents? What about Santa? Doesn't he know where to find them?"

The hard questions. Why did Santa come for some children and not others?

"He'll know where to find them," Alexandra said quietly, reassuringly.

The world seemed to go still around him as he took in the scene. He looked at Alexandra: her hair put up, the apron on, her cheeks rosy from taking the cookies from the oven. Her gaze met his, her dark brown eyes glowing with softness, light.

As long as there were people like her, pure love, there would always be someone showing Santa where to go, he realized.

His heart felt as if it would burst for loving her, for the glimpse he had been given into his own future.

This, then, was the ingredient he had missed for each Christmas where he had failed his daughter.

It wasn't about giving his daughter the perfect Christmas, but about showing her, one small step at a time, that Christmas wasn't about what you got, but about what you gave. Kindness, generosity, compassion. Even to strangers. Maybe especially to strangers.

Alexandra made him want to be a better man. A man worthy of her. He suddenly couldn't wait to bring her the joy she so willingly brought others.

He needed the perfect Christmas gift for her.

And he knew what it was going to be. A ring. But he didn't think he was going to be able to wait until Christmas to give it to her.

"What's that little smile mean?" Alexandra said, tapping his lip with the tip of her wooden spoon.

"You'll see," he promised her. "You'll see."

It was the morning of December 14. Alexandra stood in the front foyer of Parker and Parker. It was snowing lightly outside which was absolutely perfect. She had just shown the bridal party up the stairs to their private suite. Though she dealt with brides all the time, she was not sure she had ever seen one as beautiful as Ivy, radiant with love and excitement.

Now the happy chatter of the bridal party and the crinkles of bags being opened—the oohs and ahhs of rediscovering the dresses—drifted down to Alexandra.

Normally, she would feel a little ache of longing, but today her attention was already moving past the charm that ran through the entire venue. It could not look more perfect. Everything was in place.

Hailey's flowers were, as she had known they would be, extraordinary. They lent to the sense of enchantment that had been created at the beautiful mansion that sat on the edge of Central Park.

Her staff would take it from here: they would be in the background of the entire wedding, making sure that no detail was overlooked, no last-minute problems were left unsolved. Tomorrow morning they would take things down, erase it all as if it was Cinderella's glass slipper and it all disappeared at midnight.

She, herself, never attended the wedding or the reception. She never helped with the takedown. It was too difficult for her to see something she had worked on for months and months disappear in the blink of an eye, like a sandcastle dissolved by waves.

As for not attending ceremonies and receptions, at first it had been too painful for her. She had known vows exchanged, perfect days, would remind her of her own failure and trigger a deep longing in her, start a fire of yearning she would not be able to put out.

But as the years had gone by, she was not so sure if it was about that anymore. It was just that her routine had hardened into a suspicion. As if her *not* being there was part of what guaranteed great results.

Usually, on this morning, the day of the wedding, as she checked final details, as she breathed in the beauty of what had been created, she felt a sense of loss.

All weddings, but this one in particular, were all consuming. They filled her. She lived it and breathed it.

Usually, saying goodbye to it all left a yawning sense of emptiness, of what next. Usually, she was already pivoting her attention to the following wedding, to bigger and better, to yet another event that would fill any holes in her life.

But now, at the top of those stairs, the door marked Private swished open, and Drew came out. He came down the stairs, two at a time, grinning.

When had his smile become so beloved to her?

When had it become the thing that filled all those holes in her life?

He came to a stop in front of her and looked at her as if she was the only magic in this place.

"Here," he said, and he passed her a beautiful, creamy square of an envelope that reminded her of a wedding invitation.

With him watching with obvious enjoyment, she slid it open.

*The pleasure of your company is required
on the evening of December 15
at Seventh Avenue and Fifty-Ninth Street
7 p.m. at the horse-drawn carriages
Please bring swimming attire
RSVP*

"Swimming attire for a carriage ride?" Alexandra asked.

"Ah," Drew said, "be prepared to be surprised. Dress warmly."

She cocked her head at him. "Dress warmly? And bring a swimsuit?"

"That's me. I like to keep my lady on her toes."

My lady.

Even standing there in all that grandeur, Ivy and Sebastian's wedding was wiped from her mind with the ease of a note erased from a chalkboard.

She needed to find swimming attire. Nothing she had would do. She knew that. It was New York. But still, a gorgeous, sexy bathing suit in December? Was it possible?

"I have to go," she said.

"You forgot to RSVP," he called after her, evidently pleased that he had rattled her.

Well, they would just see which of them would be rattled tomorrow night!

"Yes," she called over her shoulder. "I'll be there."

Yesterday's light snow had deepened today. Alexandra arrived just before seven, a small bag over her shoulder. The new swimsuit was in the bag, and she was wearing a new, sleek black winter coat. She had on a matching set of white cashmere accessories: beret, gloves, scarf. Her staff had debriefed her about the wedding earlier in the day. It had gone perfectly. Scenes from Twitter feeds were being picked up by all the entertainment programs and media.

Still, all day, she'd had an edgy feeling. As

if something was wrong, as if she was missing something. Something important.

That feeling finally eased and then disappeared as Drew came toward her. It was as if, in the pre-Christmas crowds, she alone existed for him. He came to her, took both her hands, looked at her deeply, kissed her lightly on the mouth.

In that kiss, with huge snowflakes drifting down on them, was a white-hot promise of things to come.

He led her to a white horse-drawn carriage, delightfully decorated for Christmas. The horse blew great clouds of steam out his nostrils into the nippy air. He gave his head a shake, snow flew, and bells jingled. The carriage seat was warm under a blanket. Drew settled beside her, pulled the blanket over them, took her hand.

"Congratulations," he said. "The wedding is trending on social media. It's being compared to royal weddings."

But the truth was, it was Alexandra who felt like royalty, sitting in the carriage with her prince, the steady snow-muffled clop of the horse's hooves and the jangling of his bells like music in her ears. They were taken on the regular tour: Central Park was under a beautiful blanket of white. It was the perfect backdrop to the swirls of color and activity as they toured its most well-known sites: Wollman Rink, the carousel, the Chess and Checkers House, the Literary Walk, the boat pond and boathouse, Bethesda Fountain, the lake, Cherry Hill, and more.

And then the carriage pulled up at the walkway that was closest to Parker and Parker. In the distance it was lit up, a castle on a Christmas card.

The driver tipped his hat, and the sound of the horse clopping off and the bells faded as they took the path to Parker and Parker.

"I don't understand," she said.

"You will."

"You don't have a hot tub."

"It's New York City. Anything is possible."

The words between Alexandra and Drew had faded. All that was left was energy. Awareness. Anticipation.

They entered his private quarters, and silence greeted them.

"Where's Genevieve tonight?"

"I gave Lila some tickets to *The Nutcracker* because of her interest in theater. I told her to take anyone she wanted, but she chose to take Genevieve. They're staying at her house after. A pajama party, I understand."

Alexandra understood, too.

She and Drew were going to be alone. Uninterrupted. Tonight was the night they had been building toward since the day they had met two and a half months ago. It was as inevitable and as timeless as the changing of the seasons, as the stars coming out at night, as the tide coming in.

His hand around hers, he led her through his darkened house to his bedroom. Her heart felt like a wild bird, captured inside her chest.

He nodded. "Through there. Put on your bathing suit."

She went through to his master en suite bathroom. It was a gorgeous room. The bathtub was certainly large enough for two people.

She put on her bathing suit. She had chosen a two-piece, the first one she had ever owned. It was skimpy, red and very, very sexy. Alexandra stood staring at herself in the mirror. It seemed a different woman than who she had been two and a half months ago looked back at her.

A confident, mature woman who radiated a certainty in herself.

That's what love did.

She loved him. And she felt loved in return. And the result of that was this radiant woman who looked back at her in the mirror: sensual, sure of herself.

She stepped out of the bathroom and into the master bedroom. Two wide doors had been thrown open, and the room was already cold from the breeze coming through. She felt the freezing air and snowflakes on her bare skin.

As if in a dream, she went to those doors and stepped out. And as she did so, there was a sense of stepping into a brand-new life.

CHAPTER NINETEEN

THE MARBLE OF the deck was cold on Alexandra's
feet. Such was her state of mind that it felt delectable rather than uncomfortable. The brand-new
life that she had stepped into had a dreamlike
quality.

On the deck outside Drew's bedroom door was
a hot tub, its water softly lit, sparkling turquoise,
the steam rising off it in wispy clouds.

The entire deck was illuminated with the flickering light of what looked to be a thousand candles. They sputtered in the snow but didn't go
out. Beyond the marble balusters that enclosed
the patio area were the Christmas-lit trees of the
glade that surrounded Parker and Parker. In the
distance, even with the snowfall, the skyline of
New York was visible, soaring and illuminated.
The haunting notes of a reed flute added to the
sensation of having entered a mystical space. A
sacred one.

All that—save for the sense of the sacred—faded.

Even the impossibility of a hot tub suddenly appearing on his deck faded.

Drew was sitting on the edge of the hot tub, his feet dangling in the water. He looked as though he had been carved by Michelangelo—male perfection as snow melted on his broad chest, taut belly, sleek muscle, his flawless skin pebbled with cold.

He got up from the edge when he saw she had appeared, and stood. He was wearing a pair of slim-fitting black shorts that molded the large muscle of his thigh. He padded across the deck, leaving wet footprints, stopped and looked down at her.

She felt as if she could drown in the green depths of his beautiful eyes. She noticed the fringe of sooty lashes around them, the beginnings of whisker shadow on his cheek and chin. She felt the cold only as part of the backdrop of sensation.

Drew took his time looking, as oblivious to the cold against his naked skin as she was. He reached out his hand and swept her hair back from her face, tucked it behind her ear, then slid his thumb over and scraped it across her lips.

In the look in Drew's eyes, resting on her, Alexandra recognized that all things were possible. His hand found hers.

And he led her to the edge.

It didn't feel as if she was jumping off a cliff at all as she followed his lead and stepped into the water and felt its silky warmth close over her chilled skin.

Her sense of the sacred—of being part of the ancient dance, of one man and one woman finding each other against all odds in that endless sea of time and space—intensified.

There had been, already, so many words between them.

So much laughter.

So much shared experience.

They did not need to speak. The time for those things was not done, but it was not now. This was the time to acknowledge the other thing that had been a silent partner to their getting to know one another, shivering constantly in the background of everything else.

It was time to not just acknowledge but celebrate the anticipation that had been building between them and that was about to reach fruition.

His lips found hers. Hers found his.

They had kissed before. Light kisses. Exploratory. Rich with a sense of discovery.

But this was different. This time, unspoken, they both gave it permission to go where it wanted to go. The barriers were down.

Completely.

His mouth sighed against hers, homecoming. And then the sigh deepened. He tasted, sipped, nipped, not just her lips, but her ears, her eyelids, the hollow of her throat.

She stilled him with a fingertip and then bowed her head toward his. And she tasted, sipped, nipped, not just his lips but his ears, his eyelids, the hollow of his throat.

The exploration that began as tender and lively deepened; it took on a hunger and an urgency. They touched each other. Delighted. Discovered. Explored. Nothing taboo. Nothing forbidden. Nothing off-limits.

Bathing suits were peeled away, discarded. They surrendered to owning each other.

When both of them could barely breathe from it, Drew stood, scooped her in his arms, lifted her from the water and stepped from the tub. She watched the water slide down the beautiful planes of his face, gilded in the gold of the candlelight.

He set her down and toweled her off, following the path of the towel with his lips. She took the towel from him and toweled him off, following the path of the towel with her lips. And then he scooped her up again. Alexandra gazed into this eyes.

Drew was not a warrior claiming his prize.

He was a man, reverent, who could not believe the gift he had been given.

He took her to his bed and tenderly, fiercely, possessively, he took her to places she had not known a human being could go. He took her to the stars and to the burning center of the earth;

he took her to mossy green rocks beside bubbling brooks. He took her to exotic lands of heat and spice.

And then he rode with her to the very universal explosion where the earth began.

He stole her breath. Her heart. Her soul.

She had never felt so utterly complete. So utterly exhausted. So utterly exhilarated. It felt like the most natural and beautiful thing in the world to fall asleep with Drew whispering her name into her ear, and his arms wrapped protectively around her.

When Alexandra woke up, she was disoriented. How long had she slept? Ten minutes? An hour? Drew slept beside her, on his stomach, his arm thrown over her midriff.

But even that could not stop the anxiety from gnawing at her.

That feeling was back. More pressing than ever. That she had forgotten something. That something urgently needed her attention.

The feeling had deepened, almost as if danger lurked in a dark place just outside where her mind could touch, waiting.

She slid out from under his arm and padded quietly to the bathroom. She frowned. A phone was buzzing, and she realized it was coming from her purse.

Who would call her in the middle of the night?

And then, her heart falling like a stone, she knew. She knew what she had forgotten. Shame filled her.

And a kind of terror.

This was where passion led: to unbearable loss. To pain that seemed beyond a human's capacity to bear it.

She answered her phone.

Weeping, she quietly said hello to Brian and heard his sorrow for the baby they had buried together.

She remembered the perfect, tiny features, that one shock of golden hair like a halo. She remembered the stab of love—and loss—so sharp it had felt as if she was being cleaved in two.

And she knew a truth she had been running from since the day she met Drew. She saw the truth she had been trying to suppress as her life had opened up more and more to both him and Genevieve.

She was not strong enough to do it all again.

Not even maybe.

Drew woke up with a sense of well-being. Alexandra's scent was delicious in the air. Last night could not have gone any better. Today, his life was going to change forever. He was going to propose to the woman he loved.

He had a selection of croissants and jams. He'd make coffee, bring her a tray in bed, and on the tray he'd place the ring he had picked, a solitaire diamond. He'd known as soon as he'd seen it, it was the one. Simple, but perfect.

He turned his head to look at her, a smile of anticipation tickling his lips. Drew felt a ripple of shock and disbelief to see the place beside him was empty.

After just one night of sharing his bed with her, it felt wrong without her in it.

He listened. She must be close. Making coffee? Showering? But as he listened for those sounds, what came back to him was the hollow emptiness of no one else in the house.

He bolted from the bed, threw on pajama pants and stumbled through the house, frantic. She had to be here. Finally, back in his own bathroom, he stared at himself in the mirror.

And then he saw it.

A note, scrawled in whatever she could lay her hand to. It was lipstick, obviously, but to him it looked like blood.

I can't.

Disbelief filled him. She couldn't? After last night?

He felt the exact opposite of *I can't.*

I can.

I can give my life to you.

My heart.

My soul.

My very breath.

How could two people possibly experience the same event so differently? A sense of failure rose in him bitterly.

He thought he had done everything right. He thought back over their time together and he could not see one misstep, one moment of dissension between them.

Egotistically, he had been giving himself an A-plus in the romance department. He had thought he had aced it.

He itched to call Alexandra, to ask her what had gone wrong. Where *he* had gone wrong. But he quelled the impulse.

He might end up begging her, and no matter how you cast that argument, you could not convince someone to feel the same way you did. He went back to the bed and opened the night-stand drawer beside it. He picked up the ring and stared at it.

He was not sure he had ever felt such yawning emptiness, such powerlessness, such an agony of emotion.

No, that was not true. He had. He had, and he had ignored that poignant reminder that love brought pain. Pain so terrible it felt as if a man could not bear it.

"Daddy?"

Genevieve came noisily through the front door. Now, as then, he had to keep going for his little girl. How was he going to do it?

The shock Drew was feeling morphed into something that felt ultimately safer, and certainly more powerful. It was how he was going to do it. He was going to feel anger instead of the breaking of his own heart.

How dare Alexandra lead him on when she wasn't ready or had issues to deal with? That was one thing. But his daughter trusted her. Loved her. And that was quite another.

"Up here, sweetheart."

"'Bye, Lila," Genevieve called.

He met Genevieve outside his room, picked her up and gave her a squeeze.

"What's up, pumpkin?"

"*The Nutcracker* was the best," Genevieve said. "There were some scary parts, but I wasn't scared. There were kids in it. Can I be in it? Next year?"

Next year?

He wondered how he was going to get through the next few days and weeks, never mind next year.

"I can't wait to tell Macy about it. And Alex. I wish they could have come. I wish you could have been there, Daddy."

For a while, it had been as if they were part of a family, as if they were being invited in to all that warmth and closeness.

And now they weren't, just like that.

How did he break that to Genevieve?

"How would you like to go to California?" he said, a man desperate to outrun pain.

The trip was, predictably, a disaster. Genevieve was querulous and given to tears. She wanted to be at home. She wanted to skate again. Sled. Build snowmen. Make cookies. She wanted Alexandra.

And he did, too. For a man trying to outrun pain, he wasn't sure why he had to carry that ring around in his pocket. Touching it, holding it, feeling the warmth of it. The ring reminded him how real it had all been. How could something so real dissolve like this?

Carrying the ring made Drew hang on to some faint hope that there had been a terrible mistake. That she would call him and explain it all to him.

Every time his phone alerted, he hoped for just that. His heart hammered in his throat until he realized it wasn't the distinctive church bell tone he had assigned to her.

The bright, warm days in California blended together, and the merriment of the amusement parks and the playfulness of the beach, rather than soothing, seemed like sacrilege to him.

There was no phone call. And yet, he could not bring himself to call her. How did you argue with *I can't*? Did you insist she could? Did you insist you knew her better than she knew herself? Did you beg? Did you tell her you felt as if your world had turned to ash and cinder? What did it matter what his world was doing in the face of *I can't*?

Didn't love ask you to put the needs of another person ahead of your own? And after all that, all the time they had spent together, all the joy they had shared, she had made her decision.

And there it was.

Stark. In the note he could not bring himself to throw away, any more than he could put the ring away. The note he studied every night after Genevieve was in bed, as if some secret, some sort of answer, would reveal itself to him.

He gave up on California after just a couple days. Genevieve was not charmed by it, or distracted from her fury that Alexandra had disappeared, without explanation, from her world.

Back in New York, he made himself go through the motions of Christmas. He took her to see Santa at a department store.

"What did you ask Santa for?" he asked carefully, trying hard to hit just the right casual note to pry her secret from her.

His daughter glared at him. "I asked him for a mommy."

"Uh—"

"And I want it to be Alexandra."

And then she was weeping. He had not officially told her Alexandra would not be around anymore, trying to shield her from the pain with platitudes and distractions. But obviously she was drawing her own conclusions. The absence was weighing heavily on her. Was his lack of explanation making it better or worse?

"Let's go do our Christmas shopping," he said, trying to cajole her out of it, distract her. "You have to choose something for Lila."

The tears dried up a little bit. She perked up. "And for you. And for Macy," she said. "And for Alex."

He had warded off the tears. He wasn't going to object to any of that if it meant he didn't have to deal with a four-year-old throwing a tantrum in the middle of Macy's department store.

But as it turned out, Drew's reprieve was short. A week later, on Christmas Eve, he was exhausted from crying and tantrums. He thought it was probably exactly the wrong time to show up unannounced but hoped he could be forgiven. He was a failure at all things Christmas, after all.

With snow falling in giant flakes around him, he found himself standing in front of Shaun and Shelley's house. Genevieve was dancing excitedly beside him, the handle of a bag of wrapped gifts clutched in her fist.

When the door squeaked open, she screamed, "Merry Christmas!"

Drew wondered if he was the only one who could hear how desperate she was for exactly that.

CHAPTER TWENTY

IT WAS SHAUN who opened the door.

"Genevieve wanted to drop off these gifts for you."

Shaun took the bag that Genevieve proffered with her most angelic smile. As soon as he looked at the bag, she darted by him into the house. "Macy!"

"Sorry," Drew said.

"Not at all. Happy to have you both. To be honest, I was wondering why you haven't been around. Macy's missing Genny like crazy."

Drew scanned Shaun's face to see how much he knew, to see if he could offer a clue as to Alexandra's pulling the plug on the relationship.

He was aware Shaun was looking at him with grave sympathy.

"Man," he said, after a moment. "You look like you've been run over by a truck."

"Thanks," Drew said wryly, and thought to himself, *A truck named Alexandra.* "Genevieve picked out something for Macy, Ashley, Colin and

Michael. If you could look after getting things to Heather's girls, Adelle and Catherine, as well."

He thought of how he knew their names. Of how he had sat through each of their Christmas concerts. Of how he had begun to think of Shaun and Shelley as family. Of how he had looked forward to getting to know Heather better. He felt bereft when he thought of his life—and Genevieve's—moving on without them.

"Are you coming in?" Shaun asked.

Behind Shaun, Drew could hear the noise, Genevieve's laughter rising above it. The lights of a Christmas tree blinked on and off.

He wanted to step into that house so badly. He wanted Alexandra to be there waiting for him.

People can love too much, his aunt had warned him. He hated that. He had wanted so desperately for her to be wrong that he had overcome every survival instinct that screamed within him, and he had tried again.

"No, we'll be on our way. Genevieve picked something for your sister. If you could make sure she gets it."

"Ah, so you're not seeing her. That explains why she's even more in hiding than normal."

Drew cocked his head at Shaun. "What?" In hiding? Alexandra?

"It's unlikely I'll see her, mate."

Drew's head flew up. Somehow, he had pictured her sliding seamlessly back into the loving fold of this family. In the million reasons he'd come up with for that note—*I can't*—that had been one of them. That he was poorly equipped to give her what she wanted.

Family.

Hadn't he shared each of his failures with Genevieve? Hadn't he shown he didn't have a clue what the big family events were, never mind knowing how to celebrate them? Hadn't he fallen asleep during her nephew's Christmas concert?

"What do you mean? She'll be with you for Christmas, won't she?"

"No, she won't come. Hasn't for years."

Drew felt stunned.

"It's a bad time for her," Shaun said quietly. "We keep thinking she'll get over it, but she's got the softest heart of anyone I have ever known."

That's what Drew had thought, too. Until he'd received a note with two words on it. *I can't.*

"I think if you break her heart, it's broken for good."

Did he say this with a meaningful look aimed at Drew?

Drew wanted to explain there was little chance of him breaking Alexandra's heart, since she had beaten him to the punch.

But his mind was sluggishly turning over the fact Alexandra—expert on all things Christmas—had not celebrated with her family for years.

"The baby," Drew said, suddenly, slowly, out loud.

"You know about the baby, then," Shaun said, with a new look of appraisal. "She trusted you with that."

"What time of year did she lose the baby?" Drew's heart was thudding so loud in his ears, he thought Drew might hear it.

"This time of year," Shaun said sadly. "December 16. I can't forget it, because it's our Colin's birthday, too. A few years later. A cruel coincidence."

It felt as if the world darkened around Drew.

He had been licking his wounds. He had been making it all about him. He had been indulging his bitterness and anger.

She trusted him.

And suddenly it didn't matter to him if Alexandra loved him back. He could not bear for her to be alone with her pain. His aunt was wrong, after all. People could not love too much.

He could not love too much.

"Can you keep Genevieve for a bit?" he asked.

Shaun had the slightest smile on his face. It was approving. "You got it. Wait a sec. Take the gift from Genevieve. It might get you in the door."

Drew fished through the bag for the package with Alexandra's name on it and took off down the steps, running.

Christmas Eve, Alexandra told the stuffed green toad on her lap. *It's just another day.* Warty looked unconvinced.

She stared glumly at *Hatchets for Hallow-een*. She told herself she had chosen it only because it was the most un-Christmassy movie she could find.

She had told herself maybe it would provide a distraction from the pictures on her phone. She was afraid she was getting a permanent swipe mark on her screen from looking at them so often. Silly selfies from the hockey game. Beautiful vistas from the balloon ride.

But again and again, she went to those pictures of the perfect first day of snow in Central Park, her and Drew kissing either side of a snowman's cheek, joy shimmering in the air around them.

The movie, rather than being a distraction, reminded her of watching it with him. She loved rubbing salt in the open wound of the choice she had made to walk away. She pulled the Rangers cap down lower over her eyes, tightened the scarf she had retrieved from the snowman around her neck and cuddled Warty closer.

A choice to live without pain. For a person who had made that choice, it seemed to her she was in the most terrible pain she could have ever imagined possible.

And, worse, what if she had caused him pain? And Genevieve. It was Christmas Eve. What were they doing? Did he have a clue how to be Santa Claus? Did he know you had to put out milk and cookies? How would he know that? He had probably never done it. It was one of those things his horrible aunt would have relegated to the *nonsense* pile.

Her hand inched toward her phone, as it had done a thousand—or maybe a million—times since she had walked away. *Call him.*

The knock came on the door, loud.

Christmas Eve, she told herself bitterly. *It must be Santa Claus.* She got up, tugged back the curtain and peered out. She flipped it back down, her heart beating so hard.

"I saw you," he called. "I need to speak to you. It's urgent."

She flattened herself against the wall, trying to stop from breathing too loudly. She couldn't open that door. He would know. She was dressed in her pajamas. Her hair wasn't combed. She had on his scarf and the hat he had given her.

What a coward she was.

"It's about Genevieve."

Her self-protective mechanism abandoned her. She shoved Warty behind a flowerpot, went and threw open the door. "Drew? Is Genevieve all right?"

"No," he said, stepping into her foyer. "She's not."

This was the kind of person she was. Even worried sick about Genevieve, his scent filled her and she felt that treacherous stir of longing. "What's happened?"

"She sent this gift for you."

Alexandra's ragged breathing evened a bit. No medical emergency, then. No other child lost at this time of year when it seemed inconceivable people suffered losses. And yet they did, nursing their brokenness alone as the world celebrated around them.

"Even though you've broken her heart, still she sent a gift."

"I didn't mean to break her heart," she whispered.

"Mine, too."

"Oh, Drew, don't you see, it's better now than later?"

"I wish you would have told me," he said quietly.

She went very still.

"I wish you would have told me that December 16 was the worst day of your entire life."

"See?" she said harshly. "You think I'm someone I'm not. You want to hear the awful truth, Drew? I forgot. I was so swept away by you I forgot."

She had begun to shake. He dropped the parcel he had been holding in front of him and closed the small space between them.

He gathered her in his arms, and she wept. "I forgot," she sobbed.

"It's okay," he said over and over, his hand stroking her hair as if she was a child. "It's okay."

"It's not," she said, finally, but her voice lacked

conviction and she remained with her head pressed against the solidness of her chest.

"Maybe," he said, after a long time, "this is what love is meant to do. Make us forget. Allow us to move on. It's not time, after all, that heals all wounds, Alexandra. It's love."

"I'm scared," she admitted. "Drew, I'm so scared."

"I know."

"Not just scared. Terrified. That I will lose again. That something will happen to you. Or to Genevieve."

"It's too late," he told her softly.

"What do you mean?"

"You already love us. If something happens now, it won't matter if you're part of our lives or not. The pain will be the same. If you heard, ten years from now, I had been run over by a reindeer—"

"A reindeer?" She laughed in spite of herself, and then sighed against him.

"In honor of the season. But I digress. If you heard, ten years from now, that I had died, I think your pain would be as great as if you had spent every day of it with me."

"Is it that obvious how much I love you?" she asked.

"It is now. I'm stupid that way. I should have gotten it right away. F in the art of love. I'm willing to work to improve my grade, though. If you'll have me."

"If you'll have me, more like," she said. She tried one last time. "What if I lose another baby? I want to have babies with you. I'm so scared."

"I want to have babies with you, too."

"You do?"

"Oh, yeah. And I'm scared, too. That life has surprises for us. Not all of them pleasant. That things will not always go according to plan. That we will suffer tragedies and sorrows. But I think love gets you ready for those things. It makes you stronger every time you share a laugh, a look, a touch. It's like we'll put love in the bank to withdraw, to get us through our tough times. And life will have tough times, regardless. But we will be stronger together than we could ever be alone."

His voice was so soft she could barely hear it.

"Alexandra?"

"Yes?"

"I don't want to be alone anymore."

She was crying. She was crying because she had caused him pain, and he had come anyway. She was crying because she was afraid, but not as afraid as she had been before he was part of her life.

She was crying because life—capricious, scary, unpredictable—was, in the end, beautiful.

Mysterious.

In the end, love was everything.

"Alexandra, marry me."

"Yes," she said, and even though she said it quietly, it felt strong and loud and true. It felt like she was shouting an affirmation to life from the mountaintops. "Yes," she said again.

Alexandra, finally, the o-

"We're the right," Drew thought, she qui-
quickly fell asleep, and found a rel mad it will the
she was another an effort made to lift him the
smongstlaps. "I've," she still said it.

EPILOGUE

THEY MARRIED A year later, on December 16, to honor not the tragedy of love, but how the power of it remained in you, and carried you, through hardship. Through sorrow. Through the unexpected. Through the detours and the bumps in the road. Love was the flickering light, deep within you, that led you through darkness.

Drew and Alexandra's marriage proved his aunt wrong every single day. You could not love too much.

Nor could you use it up.

This was what Drew had learned so far. The more you loved, the more it strengthened your own light.

Once, he had hoped Genevieve would know all the things about family that he had never known.

But he did now, and so did Genevieve. Family was somebody who had your back. Family was somebody who would risk anything to bring you happiness in your darkest moment.

Though Parker and Parker was now the wedding venue of choice for all of New York City, they had not married there.

In fact, Alexandra had not wanted a traditional wedding at all. She had wrinkled her nose when Drew suggested it and said she didn't want their perfect day to feel like another day at the office for her.

She had also said no to the gown.

They had gotten married in Shaun and Shelley's snow-filled backyard, in puffy snowsuits and hats and mittens, with an honor guard of snowmen lining the "aisle."

There was no way to have a wedding party without hurt feelings if they chose Macy and Genevieve as flower girls, and so they had all of them, Genevieve and Alexandra's six nieces and nephews, as their wedding party.

And after they had said their vows, they had a snowball fight and made snow angels and drank hot chocolate and ate Christmas cookies and laughed until their stomachs hurt.

Now, as their second anniversary approached, Alexandra was pregnant. Terrified. Radiant.

Hopeful.

Above all else, the hope shone through.

It was that same hope that humanity had carried since time began: that hard times would not last forever. That tragedy would be balanced with joy. That darkness would eventually give way to light.

And that when it seemed as if it all had to fall apart, as if the whole world was disintegrating, love would be the thread that bound it all together.

* * * * *

Look out for the next story in the
A Wedding in New York trilogy

Coming soon!

And if you enjoyed this story, check out
these other great reads from
Cara Colter

His Cinderella Next Door
Matchmaker and the Manhattan Billionaire
One Night with Her Brooding Bodyguard

All available now!